THE UNSEEN

BRYAN SMITH

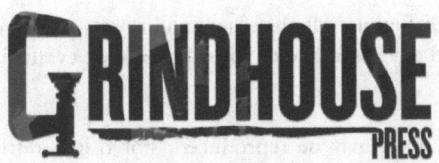

Grindhouse Press
PO BOX 521
Dayton, Ohio 45401

Grindhouse Press #080
ISBN-13: 978-1-941918-88-3

For Ryan Harding

Other titles by Bryan Smith

ONE

THE GOOD-LOOKING GUY IN the *Suspiria* shirt was still staring right at her when Allison Cook gave up pretending to look at her phone. There was nothing furtive or the least bit shy in his penetrating gaze, nor did anything perceptible change in his expression when she deliberately made direct eye contact with him.

Lustful stares from guys she didn't know was something she dealt with a lot at horror conventions. She felt eyes on her at all times whenever she came out of her room to mingle or check out the wares being peddled by various merchants in the dealer rooms. The guys were mostly too shy to give her any real problems, but now and then she was forced to fend off unwanted attention from creeps. Sometimes they followed her around or just started talking to her and kept at it even when she put out obvious vibes of disinterest and tried to move away from them. That wasn't any fun, especially when she grew impatient with them and made it clear she wanted to be left alone. A depressingly high percentage of the dudes in that category wound up calling her a bitch.

Allison tucked her phone away in a pocket of her black leather jacket and lit a cigarette. She leaned against the pillar behind her and exhaled a cloud of smoke, still maintaining eye contact. They were in the canopied area outside a side entrance of the Hyatt hotel where the convention was taking place. It was bright daylight. Several other people were hanging out in the same area with beer bottles and cigarettes in hand. She had no immediate concern of being assaulted by *Suspiria* guy. He didn't look like the type who would need to use force to get what he wanted from a woman, but that didn't always mean anything. Sometimes the good-looking ones were the worst ones. Guys in general were a crapshoot at best.

She took another draw on her cigarette, pushed away from the pillar, and walked right up to him. "So, what exactly the fuck is your deal?"

He smiled, dropping his gaze to her chest a moment before resuming eye contact. "I like your shirt."

She was wearing a tight black V-neck T-shirt with the poster art for *Friday the 13th* on the front. It was visible beneath the open front of her jacket. "You like my shirt? Really? That's the reason you're eye-fucking me so hard?"

He shrugged. "That's part of it."

"So you admit to eye-fucking me?"

He laughed and scratched the chiseled line of his jaw. It was the first gesture he'd made of anything resembling nervousness. "I guess I do."

"You guess, eh? That's a wishy-washy thing to say. Either you were or you weren't."

His smile faded. "I was."

She smirked and turned her head briefly to exhale another cloud of smoke. "That's better. Say what you mean from now on."

"Okay."

She dropped her half-smoked cigarette on the concrete and ground it out beneath the heel of her boot.

He frowned. "That's littering."

"No shit. So what's the other part of it?"

Now he looked confused. "Huh?"

She shook her head. "Jesus. You said my shirt was part of the reason for eye-fucking me. What's the other part?"

The confusion faded and his smile slowly returned. "Oh, right. You're hot. That's the other part."

Allison laughed, rolling her eyes. "Fucking hell."

It was funny. Borderline hilarious.

In her regular life, she did sometimes get similar lustful looks from men of various ages, but it was a far more common occurrence at horror cons. When she was out among the general population, she dressed in a more unassuming way. Neutral color clothing and not nearly as much makeup. She wasn't ugly, but she didn't have super-model cheekbones either. Almost a Plain Jane vibe instead. At horror cons, she allowed her inner self much more in the way of outer expression. More makeup. All-black clothing, often far sluttier than her normal attire. Today she wore black leggings. Her short nails were painted black and she had a ring in her nose she rarely wore at her administrative assistant day job.

She was "con hot", as her best friend Cassie sometimes put it. And con hot was a different thing altogether from real life hot. In regular life Allison would never consider approaching a guy this good-looking directly. Outside of the con environment, she'd dismiss him as obviously unattainable.

His expression was again tinged with confusion. "I don't get what's so funny."

She sighed. "You know what? I've been to a million of these things and I've never once hooked up with a guy at any of them, not even drunk."

He grunted, nodding slightly. "Well, that's probably smart."

She looked away a moment, scanning the faces around her. No one was watching them or showed any indication of eavesdropping on their conversation. There were no reproving glances directed her way. Her heart started beating faster as she weighed giving in to one of the wildest impulses in her life. She knew it probably wasn't the right thing to do and a part of her hoped for something to happen that would stop the idea dead in its tracks. A sudden appearance by Cassie or Julia, her roommates for the weekend, was her best hope for that, but there was no sign of them. They were either up in their third-floor room, hanging out poolside, or at the bar, or milling about somewhere else on the premises.

The good-looking guy cleared his throat in a pointed way, dragging her gaze back his way. "How big a *Friday the 13th* fan are you?"

She laughed.

That's what he wanted to talk about now? A chick he's obviously attracted to for some weird reason makes a highly suggestive remark and his comeback is something about movies? Maybe this guy was nerdier than she imagined. Some degree of nerd quotient was a given in light of that shirt and his presence here, but this was ridiculous.

She shook her head. "There is no bigger fan of the fucking

franchise than me, bub. *That's* how big a fan I am."

He chuckled. "Come on, no bigger fan?" He jerked his head in the direction of the hotel entrance. "Have you seen some of those guys? Full-sleeve *Friday the 13th* tattoos on *both* arms, some of them. Others in full Jason Voorhees regalia, complete with machete and hockey mask. Those guys *have* to be bigger fans."

Allison sneered. "Motherfucker, the Jason pillow I hug every night in bed says otherwise. I would marry Jason if I could. And how do you know I don't have just as many *Friday the 13th* tattoos? You haven't seen me out of my clothes. Yet."

There.

Let him ignore that one.

Despite her outward bravado, however, her heart rate continued to increase, and an inner admonishing voice warned her she was being far too blatantly provocative with this stranger. A man whose name she didn't even know yet.

He smiled in a more assured way now, the bold confidence he'd projected in the beginning reasserting itself. "Don't get mad. I just wanted to gauge something. What would you say if I were to tell you I have something *Friday the 13th*-related I could show you that no one else in this world has? Something that would make other *Friday* fans sick with envy if they knew about it. Hell, some of them would kill to have it. Literally."

She frowned, becoming genuinely intrigued. "Seriously? You're not just fucking with me? This isn't some line?"

He shook his head. "I don't need phony lines to pick up girls. I think we both know that."

She sighed heavily. "Okay, I give up. What is this one-of-a-kind holy grail for *Friday* freaks like me?"

The guy laughed. "No, that's not how this is gonna work." He glanced around in a wary way and dropped his voice as he leaned closer. "I can't just blurt it out in public. If you want to know what it is, you'll have to come up to my room."

Allison rolled her eyes. "Of course."

He shrugged. "Up to you. As for me, I've had enough of this heat. I'm going in." He turned away from her and moved a few steps closer to the entrance, then stopped to glance back at her. "You coming or not?"

"Up to your room?"

He nodded.

4

Her heart felt like it was almost up in her throat as she gave the matter a final moment's thought. She felt sweat on her brow and a strange tingling in her fingers. There were all sorts of good reasons for thinking it wouldn't be smart to go with this guy. She should trust her better judgment.

In the end, however, she swallowed the lump in her throat and went with him.

TWO

THEY TOOK AN ELEVATOR UP to the guy's room on the fifth floor. A full load of horror con attendees exited the elevator when its doors opened in the little open area adjacent to the lobby. Shaggy-haired guys in black horror T-shirts and girls in fishnets and skimpy outfits showing off their tattoos. In their midst was a tall, slender person of indeterminate sex cosplaying as Freddy Kreuger. Last off the elevator was a basic middle-aged couple in conservative attire who were probably from Des Moines or somewhere similar. Allison could tell from their grim expressions no one had warned them their week-end stay at the Hyatt would coincide with an event attended by freaky-looking people from all over the country.

No one else boarded the elevator with them as they stepped inside and the doors slid shut. Allison looked at the guy and smiled, her heart quickening again when he smiled back. When situations like this came up in movies, one person would grab the other and immediately engage in a passionately fierce lip-lock. An impulse to do just that came and went. A part of her absolutely wanted to be as spontaneous and daring as a character in a movie. And why not? This was one of her rare breaks from the mundane tedium of regular life. It was her right to enjoy it to the fullest and have a moment of crazy adventure. As the elevator continued to ascend, however, she realized that particular scenario would not come to fruition. Her hesitation went on a beat too long and before she knew it, the moment had passed.

The elevator stopped at no other floors on the way up and opened on the fifth-floor hallway in less than a minute. A trio of young people in swimsuits stood outside the elevators, obviously waiting to take one down to the first floor and go out to the pool. Though they wore none of the usual identifying clothes marking them as such, their horror-centric tattoos and general appearance strongly indicated they were con attendees.

The one girl in the group directed a smirking side glance at Allison as she stepped out of the elevator and moved around them. The group entered the elevator as soon as her new guy friend followed her out into the hallway. The smirking girl laughed and called out to them: "Better use protection, slut!"

The boisterous laughter of her guy friends was audible in the last moment before the doors closed.

Allison huffed as she and *Suspiria* guy continued down the hallway. "What makes that cunt think I'm randomly hooking up with you? I don't know her. For all she knows, we could be in a long-term committed relationship."

The guy shrugged. "Womanly intuition?"

Allison scowled. "Whore intuition, more like."

He chuckled. "Not my place to make that determination about any lady I don't know."

Allison gave him a dirty look. "Congratulations on your upstanding guy of the year award. You're so full of shit. What's your name?"

"Steve Miner."

They were about halfway down the hallway now.

Allison took out her phone and sent a text to Cassie: *I'm on five with some hot guy who says his name is Steve Miner.*

The whoosh of an incoming text followed shortly thereafter. Allison looked at her phone and laughed. A puke emoji followed an eye-roll emoji, followed by the words, *Tell him your good friend Sean Cunningham sez suck my fucking cock, bitch.*

Allison laughed again.

They stopped outside the door to room 526.

The guy glanced at her with a raised eyebrow as he took out his door card. "What's so funny?"

Allison looked up from her phone after sending another fast text with the room number. "What's your real name, fucker?"

He gave her a faux-innocent look. "I already told you. Steve Miner."

She shook her head. "We both know that's a lie. You didn't direct the first two *Friday the 13th* sequels."

The guy's look of fake innocence gave way to a more openly mischievous expression. "Sorry. I was testing you."

Allison raised her phone and snapped a picture of the guy's handsome face. She put it in the next text she sent to Cassie, adding, *This is the guy. We'll be in room 526.*

She tucked the phone away and looked the guy in the eye again. "Still don't believe I'm the big fan I claim to be, eh? Is it because I'm a girl?"

"Yeah."

"You motherfucker."

He laughed. "Hey, at least I'm honest."

He slipped the white door card in the card reader. The door unlocked with a loud click as the light on the reader changed from red to green. He pushed the door open and stepped into the room, turning toward her when she did not immediately follow him inside.

"Problem?"

She shrugged. "I'm not going in there until you tell me your real name. While you're at it, take out your wallet and show me your ID to fucking prove it."

He frowned. "Not a very trusting person, are you?"

She shook her head. "No, I fucking am not."

A silent moment passed as they stared at each other from opposite sides of the open doorway.

Then the guy extracted his wallet from a back pocket of his jeans. He flipped it open and showed her an Indiana driver's license, which was encased in a plastic sleeve. The ID revealed his actual name as Seth Monahan. Seth was twenty-seven as of last month. He lived in a town called Lafayette. The ID was current and not due to expire for nearly two more years.

"Satisfied?"

Allison took out her phone and snapped a picture of the ID. She sent it to Cassie and put her phone away. "Satisfied? Not yet."

She stepped into the room and kicked the door shut behind her.

THREE

THEIR CLOTHES CAME OFF IN rapid order after that and they spent right around fifteen minutes fucking on the nearest of the room's two beds. The bed closer to the window had an open old-style suitcase on it and a bunch of con loot piled up around that. Black T-shirts, books, movies, some art prints, and assorted movie-related trinkets.

After his orgasm, Seth pulled out of her and rolled onto his back, heaving a big breath. He pulled the condom she'd made him wear off his dick, tied the end of it in a knot, and tossed it away. The condom sailed across the room in a high arc and landed smoothly in the waste basket next to the dresser.

Allison sat up with her back against the headboard. "Nice shot."

Seth laughed. "In more ways than one."

Allison gave him a look of distaste. "Leave the sex puns to me. I'm better at them."

He laughed again. "If you say so. Be right back."

He hopped up from the bed and went into the bathroom, turning on the fan and partially closing the door behind him. Despite the fan, Allison faintly heard the sound of running water from the sink. He was clearly engaged in the male post-sex ritual of washing off the

9

junk. A few moments later, he came back out and resumed his position on the bed next to her.

Some silent moments passed, enough time for an uncomfortable awkwardness to take root. The initial thrill of wicked exhilaration that came with fucking a complete stranger began to dissipate shockingly fast. She was left with the disorienting knowledge that this naked person lying next to her was someone she knew next to nothing about. She knew his name and that he was good-looking and liked horror, and that was pretty much it. Dread stirred inside her at the prospect of engaging in further conversation with him. What if they talked and he revealed himself as an idiot? Maybe even the kind of guy who spent the bulk of his time on the dumbest right-wing conspiracy forums on the internet. Jesus, how depressing would that be? She already knew he harbored some sexist tendencies, which was a pretty reliable warning sign when it came to that kind of thing.

Seth cleared his throat in a way that suggested he too was keenly aware of the awkwardness of the moment. "So, uh . . . who were you texting before you came in here?"

She looked at him. "My friend Cassie. Why? Does that bother you?"

He frowned, shrugging. "Well . . . kind of. Looked like you sent her that picture of my ID."

"I sure did."

"Yeah, but why?" His frown deepened as he sat up and put his back against the headboard. "I mean, there's a lot of sensitive information on a driver's license. For all I know, you guys might be identity thieves."

Allison laughed. "That picture was my insurance against winding up strangled in a ditch somewhere. It means you can't murder me without having the police on your ass in no time."

"I have no intention of murdering you."

"How fortunate for me."

Another awkward silence stretched out.

Allison took another look around the room as she began contemplating how she might make a relatively quick but graceful exit from this situation. The room was a slovenly mess. In addition to the clothes in the open suitcase, there were more garments strewn across the floor. Empty or partially empty beer cans and bottles occupied every surface. Evidently he'd also come to the con with roomies. Or he'd found one or more random people to party with him last night.

Either possibility was just as likely. Not that she actually cared either way.

She was about to start reaching for her clothes when she thought of something. "Oh, hey. What was that one-of-a-kind thing you wanted to show me? You said it was something to do with *Friday the 13th*?"

Seth's expression had turned dour, but now he managed a tentative smile. "Oh, yeah. Um . . . there's just one thing, though. Something we need to agree on first."

"And what would that be?"

A solemness entered his voice as he said, "You have to swear you'll never breathe a word of it to anyone. Seriously. Not anyone. *Ever.*"

She spent a moment studying his expression for signs of subtle playfulness, but detected nothing of the sort. Despite her doubtful instincts, she found herself becoming truly intrigued. She thought it highly unlikely this guy possessed any *Friday* artifact genuinely worthy of holy grail status, but it was at least remotely possible he owned something cool. Maybe a movie-used prop with a certificate of authenticity. Something like that. Whatever the case, she was unlikely to ever see this dude again, so there was no harm in telling a little white lie.

She put a hand to her chest and raised the other hand in the air. "I'll never breathe a word of it to anyone. I swear it on Pamela Voohees' grave."

Seth's smile became less guarded after that. "Good enough."

He got off the bed and pulled on his boxers.

Then he went over to the suitcase, reached into the sleeve on the back side of the lid, and pulled out a videotape. The tape's thin cardboard case was worn and frayed around the edges. On the side of the tape was a white label with faded handwritten letters, only a few of which Allison could make out due to the placement of Seth's hand.

F-R-I.

That's what she saw.

She leaned forward and wrapped her arms around her knees as she pulled them closer to her chest. "Ooh, am I about to see some supposedly rare lost footage?"

He smiled. "Not exactly. It's something much more substantial than that. There's really no point in describing it beforehand. Just watch."

The room's modern flatscreen TV was pushed up against the wall behind the dresser. Situated in front of it was one of those old TV/VCR combo units. Real vintage tech. She had a few VCRs of her own back home. They were a necessity for anyone interested in building a respectable library of old VHS tapes. Okay, so maybe she didn't technically need more than one, but digging into the process of acquiring that stuff was like getting hooked on crack.

Seth inserted the videotape in the slot beneath the combo unit's small screen. He grabbed a remote and took a seat on the edge of the mattress at the foot of the bed. After a moment's hesitation, Allison joined him there.

He glanced at her, his expression turning serious again. "I meant what I said, okay? You seriously can't tell anyone about this. If knowledge of it got out, there could be some pretty bad consequences."

Allison frowned and shifted a few inches to her right, deliberately putting a little more separation between them. "Are you threatening me?"

His eyes widened and his mouth dropped open in a look of almost comical shock. "God, no. Jesus. I just have to be really careful when it comes to showing this to anyone. Hell, I shouldn't be doing it at all, but . . . well, I like you. And you're such a big fan. And we just *did* it. I really want you to see this, but I have to feel sure about it."

Allison sighed.

It'd been a long time since she'd heard any guy—especially a guy who looked like this one—sound so dopily earnest about anything. She had no doubt now the concern he was expressing was genuine, which was reassuring on one level, but it also had the effect of massively amping up her sense of intrigue.

"Seth, I give you my word. You can trust me, okay?"

He studied her face a moment longer before nodding.

Then he aimed the remote at the TV/VCR combo and pushed PLAY.

FOUR

THE FIRST THING TO APPEAR on the little screen was a field of white static. This was soon replaced by a rolling picture, something she frequently saw on old recordable videotapes where people had taped things from television broadcasts. That was another thing she was into collecting, frequently buying them in lots of ten or more. It was fun to go through them and see cheesy old commercials and news breaks between segments of sitcoms and cop shows. She loved it when the newscasters talked in their very serious news voices about apparently important matters that happened before she was even born.

Seth aimed the remote at the device and adjusted the tracking.

Within a few seconds, the recorded images stopped rolling. Some blur and fuzz remained, but there was nothing to be done about that. This was clearly a tape of advanced age. Whatever she was about to see must've been recorded multiple decades in the past. The images on the screen kept shifting. Different actors, different settings and situations. In a few more seconds, she realized she was seeing a number of quick clips from various old movies. A few she recognized, but many others were unknown to her. Obscure and possibly once popular movies now faded from the memories of all but a few. Orchestral music accompanied the images. This was undoubtedly some manner of general promo video for some cable movie channel.

Then the images disappeared and were replaced by a white HBO logo against a dark background. It was notably similar to the network's modern logo, but was different in some subtle ways. The logo rotated against a field of moving stars, an animation that soon yielded to the words HBO FEATURE PRESENTATION.

The screen went black again.

Seth tapped another button on the remote a few times and a green volume level indicator appeared at the bottom, stretching rapidly toward the right of the screen. In that moment, most of what Allison was feeling was mild bemusement. Her expectations regarding whatever she was about to see were not high. Despite Seth's ominous insinuations, she doubted there would be anything particularly revelatory on this tape. Certainly nothing that would make it dangerous or illegal to own. Well, okay, maybe a bit illegal if it turned out this was, say, some bootlegged workprint of one of the original eight installments in the *Friday* franchise, but even then the fucking FBI wouldn't be kicking in anyone's door over it. Seth was just one of those guys who liked to brag and talk big. Nothing more to it.

That impression remained intact for only a few more seconds.

The first goosebumps popped up on her arms the instant she heard the first notes of what was recognizably a Harry Manfedini musical score. These notes were immediately followed by the iconic *ki ki ma ma ma* soundtrack whispers familiar to all fans of the *Friday* movies. The black screen soon gave way to a scene of young people gathered around a campfire in the woods at night. They were laughing and cutting up, drinking beers and passing around a joint. This went on for only a few moments. Typical scene establishment stuff.

Then one of the guys abruptly took charge of the conversation, telling everyone else to pipe down. When he had their attention, he launched into an account of the legend of Jason Voorhees. The things he said were intercut with brief scenes from various *Friday the 13th* installments, mostly quick kill shots. She was strongly reminded of the almost identical opening sequence to *Friday the 13th Part IV: The Final Chapter*. It differed from that sequence in that it also included quick clips from movies that followed *The Final Chapter*.

In particular, scenes from *Jason Lives* and *Jason Takes Manhattan*.

Also, she recognized none of the actors in this campfire scene rehash, but of course that made perfect sense, because she believed she understood what she was seeing now. These actors were unfamiliar because they were not Hollywood professionals. They were, instead, enthusiastic and committed amateur performers hired by whoever had put together this—so far, at least—skillfully staged fan film.

Because of the long-standing dearth of new official films in the franchise, an abundance of amateur films produced by passionate fans desperate to fill the void had flourished over the last decade, frequently racking up hundreds of thousands of views on YouTube. They ranged in quality from unwatchable trash to more ambitious productions that were close to professional level.

It was early yet, but this one looked more promising than most, despite its obvious lack of storytelling originality. Another thing she liked about it was the way it'd been made to look like something recorded off cable TV long ago. That was an obvious production design choice rather than anything actually vintage. Even she'd been fooled initially, which wasn't easy to do.

She gave Seth a suspicious sidelong glance. Hell, for all she knew, he was the filmmaker, and everything leading up to watching this tape was just his idea of creative showmanship.

He frowned when he looked at her. "Whatever you're thinking, it's wrong. Trust me."

She laughed. "Yeah. Okay."

"I'm serious." He nodded at the screen, the look on his face as earnest as ever. Maybe even a touch exasperated. "Keep watching."

She sighed and decided to humor him a while longer.

Her attention returned to the screen.

The scene cut away from the campfire to a shot of the dark surface of what she guessed was supposed to be Crystal Lake at night. The murky water was calm. There were insect sounds in the background. Then came a few quieter notes from the ominous score, which she assumed was a digitally assembled hodgepodge gathered from various pieces of Manfredini's official scores. A breath bubble appeared on the surface of the lake, rippling outward. The scene cut to two pairs of bare legs hanging over the end of a pier. One pair was hairy, the other smooth and hairless. A young man and woman making out as more breath bubbles appeared in the water below them. The man reached a hand inside his girlfriend's blouse.

Allison smiled.

Despite her cynicism, she was getting a bit excited. She couldn't wait to see the Jason impersonator surge up out of the water with his machete. Hopefully the demise of the couple on the pier would involve some decent gore FX. It wouldn't be Tom Savini level, of course, but some of those amateur effects artists could come up with some pretty great stuff.

Jason did rise up out of the water in a few more seconds. The young couple scrambled backward as he stepped up onto the pier and went to work with his machete. Two heads flew into the air one after the other, both subsequently striking wood and rolling toward the opposite end of the pier. Moments later, the faces of the severed heads stared up at the sky as Jason loomed over them. The camera shot was from ground level, making the undead killer look like a giant. Then came a close-up shot of Jason's bulging, red-rimmed eyes behind the beat-up old hockey mask. He was breathing heavily. His anger was palpable as he raised a booted foot and squashed the heads flat one by one.

Allison gasped. "Holy shit."

Seth chuckled.

The gruesome FX work was far superior to anything she'd expected, but that was only the second most shocking thing about what she'd just seen. The *most* shocking thing was the face of the actor who'd portrayed the young male victim. He was a dead ringer for Ryan Laettner, the long-time A-list superstar who was still often in the news for one thing or another. There was no doubt in her mind this was him, albeit the way he'd looked at the start of his career as opposed to now.

But Ryan Laettner had never appeared in a *Friday the 13th* film, nor was there any way in hell he'd ever deign to appear in anything so beneath him as a mere fan film.

The screen went black again.

There was a moment of almost tranquil quiet.

Then the classic *Friday the 13th* logo from the first film in the franchise appeared in the bottom right-hand corner of the screen. Music swelled as the logo increased in size, rising to fill the middle of the screen. Then, in an obvious call-back to *Part II*, the logo exploded, only once again to be replaced by a black screen. Next came multiple slashing sounds as the following appeared in jagged red letters, like blood leaking from the black background:

PART IX

HOMECOMING

Another fade to black followed.

Then daylight and the start of a scene of young people in a jeep, laughing as they traveled along a tree-shrouded rural road. Two faces in this scene were familiar ones right off the bat. One belonged to someone still well-known, while the other was the face of a genre actor who'd faded from the scene long ago.

Allison stared at the screen in silent shock a moment longer.

Then she huffed out a breath and looked at Seth. "What the fuck?"

FIVE

THE LOOK ON HIS FACE was so deeply smug she couldn't stand it. He probably wouldn't be smirking like that if he knew how close the sight of it brought her to the brink of an act of impulsive violence.

Instead of assaulting him, she snatched the remote from his hand and hit the pause button. At this early stage in the film, credits were still appearing on the screen as the first post-opening sequence played out. When she paused the scene, it happened to stop on a credit that read: SPECIAL MAKEUP FX BY TOM SAVINI.

She stared at those words a moment, waiting for them to disappear or morph into something else, revealed as a trick of her imagination, but that didn't happen. The words stayed right there.

Allison looked at Seth. "*Someone* went to a lot of trouble to make this look like a legit original period *Friday* sequel."

The extra emphasis on 'someone' left no doubt to whom she was referring.

Seth's smirk vanished. "I get what you're thinking and I can't blame you for it, but I had nothing to do with making this film. It's not even possible, because I wasn't born yet when it was made."

A corner of Allison's mouth curved sharply upward. "Bullshit."

Seth shook his head. "No bullshit. This thing *is* legit. I'll swear to it on a stack of bibles. Or whatever your religious text of choice is."

Allison's sneer deepened. "I'm an atheist, you fuck. That doesn't mean shit to me."

Seth winced at her tone. "Why are you always so harsh? I'm just trying to share something cool with you."

She laughed. "You're trying to pull one over on me. That's what you mean. How fucking stupid do you think I am?"

He sighed. "I don't think you're stupid at all. A little mean, but not stupid. And a smart girl like you is obviously gonna be skeptical about something like this. But you gotta admit, what you've seen so far is fucking indistinguishable from the real thing. And the reason for that is simple. It *is* the real thing."

Allison's gaze returned briefly to the frozen image on the screen, which was an up-angle shot of the person behind the wheel of the jeep. The actor playing that character was one of the two recognizable faces in the scene. He was the slightly more famous of the two. She'd even met him at horror cons a few times. At one of them she'd purchased a black-and-white signed headshot from him. It was currently in a frame on one of her shelves back home.

A thought occurred to her, something that might well explain one of the more inexplicable aspects of what she'd seen so far. When she looked at Seth again, she was smiling rather than smirking. "The scenes with the name actors is deep-fake stuff, isn't it? You've used that technology to superimpose their faces over the faces of unknown performers. And the artificially degraded quality of the tape smooths over any signs of trickery." She laughed and shook her head, reaching over to pat Seth on the knee. "You motherfucker. You almost had me fooled."

Seth winced again.

The tap on his knee was a little harder than she'd intended.

He gave her an exasperated look. "Trust me, I'm not nearly talented or knowledgeable enough to pull off any of the shit you keep accusing me of. All I can say is keep watching. It won't be long before you see I couldn't possibly have made this myself. I'd need at least a million bucks to even try."

Allison shrugged. "So maybe you're a spoiled brat with an indulgent rich daddy. Or sugar daddy. You're good-looking enough."

Seth's expression darkened. "You've got an explanation for everything, don't you? Do you want to watch the rest or not?"

Allison pursed her lips, thinking about it. "Hold on."

She dropped the remote and scooted away from him to lean over the side of the bed, snatching her jacket up from the floor long enough to extract her phone from one of its pockets. Still leaning over the side of the bed, she looked at the screen and saw she'd received several texts from Cassie and one from Julia. They were out by the pool now and wanted her to come join them.

"How long is this fucking fake-ass movie?"

Seth cleared his throat. "Ninety-three minutes. Right around average for the franchise."

Allison rolled her eyes.

She sent a text to Cassie: *Give me a bit yet. Dude is showing me something.*

Cassie's quick reply: *I bet.*

Allison sat up again.

She scooted closer to Seth, but not as close as before. He'd commandeered the remote again. "Roll this shit back a bit," she told him. "To right before the titles start."

He frowned. "Why?"

"Just fucking do it."

The sour look on his face strongly indicated he was tiring of her attitude, but he did as she asked anyway. As soon as he hit play again, she snapped two quick pictures with her phone. One showed the *Friday the 13th* logo in the moment just before it exploded. The second showed the subtitle of the fake sequel. She put both pictures in a text to Cassie and hit send.

"Whoa, whoa, whoa." There was a note of what sounded like genuine alarm in Seth's voice. He hit the pause button again, this time freezing the screen on an exterior shot of the jeep traveling down the rural road. "What are you doing?"

She raised an eyebrow as she glanced at him. "You saw what I did. I sent the pictures to my friend."

He gaped at her in silent disbelief for an extended period.

"What's the problem, Seth?"

He made a sound of deep incredulity. "Oh, nothing. You only just broke the promise you made multiple times not to speak of this to anyone. Like, right in front of me, without even trying to hide it."

She stared at him a moment, her face devoid of expression.

He looked actually hurt by her little betrayal, a feeling writ large in the pinched set of his features.

She scooted closer to him and slipped a hand inside his boxers.

He sighed, glancing at her. "Really? I just blew my load a few minutes ago. Do you really think that's gonna distract me . . . sorry, I just realized you never told me your name."

Her hand curled lightly around his cock, squeezing gently. "It's Dana." She squeezed again. "Dana Kimmell. And who knows, maybe by the end of the movie you'll feel up to making me scream again."

Despite his protest, the anger and hurt was gone from his voice and expression now. "You really want to watch the rest of it?"

"I really do. Real or fake, it's amazing so far. And who knows, maybe it'll be like you say—by the end I'll have no choice but to believe."

He studied her face a moment before shrugging. "Okay."

He hit the play button on the remote and the movie resumed.

Her hand remained inside his boxers for nearly the remainder of the movie, eventually bringing him back to the point of arousal. She felt the first twitch of his cock after more than thirty minutes of slow manipulation. His breathing deepened and he leaned back slightly, but she maintained her light touch. The physical ministrations occurred on a disconnected level while the majority of her focus remained on the events unfolding on the screen. She heard him whimper a time or two, however, and knew she was subjecting him to an exquisite form of torture by way of deprivation.

Served him right for being so annoying earlier.

On the screen, a story adhering to many of the slasher film norms of the 1980s unfolded in semi-predictable but unexpectedly thrilling fashion. Though it did a lot of the same things as those movies, here the pacing was tighter and the dialogue far sharper than usual. The screenplay was credited to a man she knew was a veteran horror novelist, one of the originals of the 80s splatterpunk era. Of course she figured this was another false credit, but *someone* had done a damn fine job, probably better than the material actually deserved.

The gory moments were plentiful and came at a faster rate than in any of the original entries in the *Friday* series. The kills were often creative and shocking, delivered in the form of masterful practical effects. Maybe Tom Savini hadn't actually created these effects, but they were certainly worthy of comparison to his best work. Work like that didn't come cheap. Nor did the lavishly staged crash of a semi-trailer during the highway getaway sequence toward the end. The basic concept of the movie was that Jason had returned home to Crystal Lake after his excursion to Manhattan, thus the subtitle. A simple tale stunningly executed. She was entranced throughout and even before it was over she knew it was her favorite *Friday the 13th* movie since *The Final Chapter*. Legit franchise movie or not.

In truth, by then she was no longer as certain in her assumptions.

Only once the end credits began to roll did reality begin to come back into focus. Seth was moaning and whimpering continuously, his rigid cock throbbing in her grip. She looked at him and had to stifle a laugh. His face was sheened in sweat. Tears glimmered in his eyes. Such a weak boy.

He gasped when she took her hand out of his boxers.

He trembled when he looked at her. "Why did you do that?"

She replied with a question of her own. "You can wait a minute. What's the deal with this movie?"

His brow furrowed. "Huh?"

She ignored him and said, "It really feels like a legit vintage *Friday* movie. I mean, I can't fucking believe it, but that's what my gut is telling me. Was it produced in secret and never released for some reason? Then maybe it stayed in a vault forever after New Line acquired the rights to the franchise? Something like that?"

Seth huffed in frustration after struggling to swallow a lump in his throat. "It's nothing like that. The truth is way more complicated. But it's one-hundred percent a real *Friday the 13th*."

Allison grunted. "Okay. So enlighten me. Explain how that's possible."

Seth hesitated a moment.

Then he took hold of her hand and guided it back over to his crotch. He looked at her expectantly and said nothing.

Her face crinkled. "I don't feel like fucking you again."

"But you said—"

She grunted. "I know what I said. I changed my mind. That's my right, you know."

"Whatever. Then just jerk me off."

She sighed. "Fine."

Her hand went back inside his boxers and she made him come in under a minute. She removed her hand and wiped it thoroughly on the bed sheet. After Seth's moaning and shuddering ceased, he got up and went into the bathroom again, once again closing the door and turning on the fan. Only this time he pushed the door all the way into the frame, until it clicked shut.

Allison sat on the edge of the mattress for about three more seconds.

Then an idea took hold of her.

A wild impulse she couldn't deny.

She went to the TV/VCR combo, pressed the eject button, and held her fingers against the tape slot as the machine worked to expel the tape. This had the effect of significantly muting the ejection process, with the tape nudging up against the slot flap instead of popping through it. She opened the tape slot and removed the movie.

As soon as she had the tape, she went into a flurry of urgent motion, pulling on her clothes, boots, and jacket as rapidly as she could manage. All this took less than two minutes. The bathroom's fan was still running as she went to the door of the room. Her hand was turning the knob as she heard the fan click off.

Allison's heart pounded as she hauled the door open and raced down the hallway.

SIX

MARK CASTLEBERRY LEFT HIS SOILED underpants on the tiled bathroom floor as he opened the door and stepped back out into the room. No big deal. The chick had already seen him naked. Hell, she'd had his dick inside her. Maintaining any false pretense of modesty was pointless.

Once he was out of the bathroom, the girl's absence took a moment to fully register. He stared at the empty spot on the mattress where she'd been sitting, squinting in confusion. A quick glance around the messy room confirmed she hadn't simply moved elsewhere within it.

She was *gone*.

Unless she was hiding in the closet or under one of the beds for some mysterious reason, but that would be silly. Then again, some girls liked to do silly, impulsive things. She might be messing with him, waiting for him to start freaking out, at which point she'd reveal herself and laugh at him. They'd both laugh at how she'd made him look like an idiot.

He in no way believed this was a serious possibility. This was just his mind spinning off in ridiculous directions in the absence of an actual explanation for her disappearance. The more likely reason for her departure was more depressing. She'd had her fun with him and now wanted nothing more to do with him. He hated to admit it, but in truth it was something he'd started sensing almost immediately after they did it. She had this bored look in her eye that only went away once they started watching *Homecoming*.

Just up and vanishing like this was plain rude, even if she had no interest in him beyond sharing a one-time sexual experience. Mark was self-aware enough to know he was good-looking. He had no trouble attracting women. Keeping their interest, however, was another story. Girls tended to find him off-putting after not very long. It hurt his feelings a lot because he was always nice to them. Or tried to be at least.

In his twenty-four years on earth (the age on his phony driver's license was a lie), he'd had exactly one honest-to-gosh girlfriend, one willing to hang out with him longer than a few weeks before either ghosting him or telling him to fuck off. He still missed Cynthia. They were together almost ten whole months. When she abruptly left him two years ago, he was despondent, crying almost continuously for weeks on end. That was such a bad time. He thought a lot about killing himself.

Only the constant background presence of The Visitor made any of it bearable. The Visitor was an interdimensional psychic parasite but also a sharer of secret knowledge. Things about the malleable and multifarious nature of existence itself. The Visitor was also a bearer of precious and inexplicable gifts. In Mark's case, these were mostly pop cultural artifacts, impossible movies whose existence ran counter to what he knew as established and undeniable media history.

Yet they did exist. In some other somewhere.

Homecoming was far from the only such artifact in Mark's possession. His bedroom closet back home in Illinois was filled with similar treasures. All thanks to The Visitor. And until today he'd never once shown any of them to a stranger.

For good reason.

The Visitor called the inexplicable treasures "gifts", but they were less innocent than that word suggested. Possession of them came at a price.

A steep one.

It was just as well, really, that the girl hadn't stuck around. Otherwise, having let her see *Homecoming*, he might have been forced into attempting to explain things he didn't fully understand. Once he got past the momentary sting of rejection, he found that being spared that extra level of awkwardness was actually something of a relief. Now he could just relax and get on with enjoying the rest of the con.

Or . . . wait.

He turned around and stared at the TV/VCR unit, frowning as he thought about how Dana had slipped out of his room without making a single sound, at least none he could hear while in the bathroom. Making that perfectly noiseless an exit didn't seem possible. Most people would make some kind of audible sound by accident. By bumping into a table or chair on the way out of the room, maybe, or by dropping their keys. Or any number of other things. The manner of her exit implied stealth and cunning.

Oh, shit.

Mark began to have a sick feeling in his stomach.

He punched the TV/VCR's eject button.

Nothing happened.

Oh shit, oh shit, oh shit!

He pushed the tape slot's flap in and looked inside the device.

Empty.

"Fuuuuuuuuuuuuuccck! You fucking bitch!"

He slammed the base of a fist against the top of the dresser. A molten rage erupted inside him as his face turned red and his hands clenched into shaking fists. He began flinging himself around the room, punching his fists against the walls hard enough to draw blood from his abraded knuckles. Hard enough to put dents in the walls. He tore off one of the wall-mounted lamps above the bed and frenziedly smashed it to pieces. Tossing the remains of the lamp aside, he grabbed an empty beer bottle and smashed it against the mirror behind the dresser.

He couldn't believe she'd stolen the goddamn movie. Something he'd shown her in kindness, out of the goodness of his heart. And how had the deceitful little whore repaid that act of selfless generosity? By stealing his treasure from him the first chance she got.

You fucking goddamn whore!

An image of his hands wrapped tight around her slender neck came unbidden into his head. An image so real he could almost feel her windpipe collapsing beneath the crushing force of his squeezing hands. He ached with every fiber of his being to make the image reality.

He screamed again and ran to the door, yanking it open and stepping out into the hallway. His head snapped fast in both directions, but there was no sign of her anywhere. She'd made good her getaway while he was busy being clueless and then raging about inside the room. So far everything was going her way. Well, that was going to change.

One way or another, by God, it was going to damn well change.

Before he could retreat into his room, the door on the opposite side of the hallway opened and a thirty-ish woman dressed as Patty Mullen from *Frankenhooker* soon stood framed in the open doorway. She gasped and froze in place with her mouth wide open when she got a look at him. In the midst of his rage, he hadn't thought to put on his clothes before rushing out to check the hallway. He didn't have a stitch on. Something about this stranger seeing him exposed like this in a public area further fueled his already volcanic rage. The woman must have seen something in his eyes that scared her, because she immediately backed into her room and slammed the door shut. He heard the lock sliding into place an instant later.

Mark backed into his own room and closed the door.

He grabbed some clothes from his open suitcase and dressed in a hurry.

Then he took an elevator down to the first floor to search for the thief.

SEVEN

THE ELEVATOR STOPPED TWICE ON the way down to the ground floor. Multiple people got on at each stop, their attire identifying most of them as convention attendees. Both times Mark needed every ounce of will he could summon not to scream in frustration. He had no clue what the thieving bitch's next move would be, but he couldn't help feeling time was of the essence.

Any hope of recovering the tape hinged on tracking her down fast, before she could leave the hotel and flee to some unknown destination, a prospect that filled him with dread and more than just a little existential terror. People at the convention were from all over the country, and not once during their brief time together had he thought to ask her where she was from. Her accent was undoubtedly some form of North American, but not in any distinct regional way he could pin down. She might end up almost anywhere.

When the elevator opened on the ground floor, Mark roughly pushed his way through the people in front of him, ignoring their angry cries of protest as he strode rapidly out to the lobby. He came to a stop in the approximate center of the large, open space and took a slow look around. Beyond the lobby was a small cafe. To the right of that was a wide hallway leading to the celebrity and dealer rooms. A steady stream of people trickled in and out of that area. Lots of other people were hanging out in the spacious lounge adjacent to the lobby. He searched the faces he saw to no avail.

There was no sign whatsoever of Dana.

Not that he'd expected to find her so easily. She wouldn't just be lounging about out in the open after stealing a rare commodity from another con attendee. Glancing over at the reception desk, he caught the eye of a young woman behind the counter. A cute brunette who couldn't be any older than maybe twenty. She was staring at him even before he turned in her direction, which did not surprise Mark. He was six feet tall and skinny, with a face that might've made him famous had he possessed any variety of talent worth celebrating, which he did not. Girls stared at him all the time.

Putting on his best smile, he sauntered his way over to the desk and leaned over the counter. "Hey there."

The girl blushed. "Hey."

Mark's gaze flicked to the name tag pinned to her blouse. "You're really cute, Tina. Anyone ever tell you that?"

Her blush deepened and she laughed a little. "Sometimes, I guess."

He chuckled and increased the wattage of his smile. "Oh, I bet it's more than just sometimes. Listen, I was wondering if you could help me out."

"I'll try my best," she said brightly, clearly enjoying the flirtatious interlude, which was probably a nice break from dealing with cranky guests, most of whom likely weren't nearly as pleasing to the eye as he was.

Still leaning over the counter, he craned his head around to survey the vicinity again.

Still no sign of the thief.

Mark looked at the cute desk clerk. "Have you been behind the desk here continuously for . . . oh, let's say, the last twenty minutes or so? Without ducking into an office or anything?"

She thought about it only a second or two before nodding. "Oh, yeah, definitely. Maybe more like thirty minutes."

He leaned back a little and said, "Oh, awesome. Great. I'm looking for a friend of mine. This really cute girl." He saw the clerk's smile slip slightly and knew he needed to hurriedly amend what he'd said. "She's not my girlfriend or anything. I'm single." He chuckled in a forced way that made her frown. *Shit, I'm losing her.* "Anyway, I think she might have come through here. She'd be really hard to miss.

Dressed all in black with a leather jacket. Has blonde hair almost to her shoulders with, like, these black tips. Wearing a *Friday The 13th* shirt. What I'm wondering is, did you see her leave the hotel? We were supposed to meet up here in the lobby."

Tina looked at him blankly a moment. "You sure this isn't someone you're trying to hook up with?" Her frown returned. "Or stalking?"

Mark laughed in what he hoped was a reassuring way.

Inwardly, however, he was raging again.

The nerve of this bitch, talking to him this way. Her job was to stand behind that goddamn counter and answer any questions put to her, not make shitty insinuations for no good reason. He wanted to grab her by the throat and make her apologize, but that wouldn't get him anywhere, other than maybe in jail. *Someone* should put her in her place, though. He made a mental note to put in a complaint to the manager prior to his departure from Virginia. He'd have to embellish his account of the incident, make her sound way ruder than she actually was.

"It's nothing like that, I swear. This chick wouldn't want to fuck me anyway. She's a dyke."

Tina winced.

Mark realized his often faulty verbal filter had failed him once again. "Oh, shit. Sorry. I honestly didn't mean that as a slur or anything. She describes herself that way all the time and I guess it's kinda rubbed off on me. But that's no excuse. I've got no right to say that kind of thing."

God, he hated how smarmy his voice sounded to his own ears.

How *placating*.

She held his gaze a moment longer, doubt about him still in her eyes, but then she appeared to relax some. "Yeah, I have some friends like that." She glanced around, checking to see if anyone was listening. "Black friends. They're always throwing that one word around. You know what I mean."

Mark nodded. "The N-word."

"That's the one. I get so used to hearing it, I slip and say it myself sometimes. People get all pissy when a white girl does it. It's not fair." She sighed. "Anyway, a lot of those horror chicks have come through here, but definitely not that one."

Mark cocked his head to one side and raised an eyebrow. "Definitely? How can you be so sure?"

"Because I saw your friend when I came in this morning. She was smoking a cigarette out front. Matched your description exactly." A troubled look crossed her face. "Stuck in my mind because she looked right at me and gave me what I thought was a mean look, but now that I know what she is . . ." She glanced around, then dropped her voice again. "Maybe she was just, you know, checking me out."

Mark shrugged. "Could be. You kind of look like her type."

He thought the clerk's first impression of Dana was likely much closer to the truth. For one thing, the bitch was into guys. That was pretty obvious, given what transpired between them prior to her disappearance. Also, she had a deeply surly nature. He had a hunch a high percentage of strangers who made direct eye contact with her thought she was giving them a mean look, when it was actually just her default expression.

Anyway, he'd probably learned about all he could from Tina. The thief hadn't exited the hotel through the lobby. Probably. It wasn't much, but it was better than knowing nothing at all.

He pushed away from the counter. "Thanks for your help."

The girl's face dropped, crushing disappointment evident in her eyes. "But—"

"See ya."

He moved again into the center of the lobby, took another look around at the horror people passing by in all directions, and decided to take a shot in the dark. "I'm looking for Dana Kimmell!" He raised his voice considerably, instantly turning a number of heads in his direction. This was good. Maybe he'd get a real lead on the bitch sooner than he feared. "She's about yay high." He held a hand up at about the level of his shoulders and waggled it. "Or thereabouts. Young. Blonde hair with black ends. Wearing a leather jacket and a *Friday the 13th* shirt."

A lot of glances were exchanged among those who'd stopped to listen. There were some smirks on those faces, which Mark found confusing. Then came the splutters of laughter and his face reddened with anger.

"What's so fucking funny?"

A big brown-skinned man in a shirt identifying him as con staff was standing nearby. He was one of the smirking ones. He moved a little closer and said, "Okay, pal, first of all, Dana Kimmell isn't booked here this weekend. Scheduling conflict. Secondly, she looks nothing like the young lady you described. I suspect you were given a false name by a smart woman who wanted nothing to do with your belligerent ass."

Mark stood there stewing in confused anger perhaps five more seconds.

Then it came to him.

Oh, you lying cunt.

Dana Kimmell was the name of the lead actress in *Friday the 13th Part III*.

How had he not thought of that?

His failure to connect the alias she'd used with the *Part III* actress was the fault of his trusting nature. He had a blind spot where girls were concerned in that area. It simply never occurred to him to think "Dana" wasn't being truthful about things during their brief time together. He was certain he would've made the connection much sooner—perhaps even instantaneously—had he been on a higher state of mental alert.

The laughter of the onlookers followed him as he put his head down and angrily stalked out of the lobby. He did a circuit of the crowded celebrity and dealer rooms, pushing his way through the throngs of costumed cosplayers and black T-shirt-wearing fans. His brusque manner drew lots of complaints, but he ignored them all, even when he got the occasional hard shove in return. The object here was to find the nameless bitch, not get in a fight with some random jerkoff. Because the rooms were so big and crowded, it took a solid twenty minutes to fully work his way through them, even at this accelerated pace.

There was no sign of the thief.

Fuck.

He went out to the pool area and looked there, too.

Same result.

Motherfucker!

He was getting nowhere in a hurry. Precious time was ticking away and his chances of recovering the tape were dwindling. He needed to go back to his room and do some serious thinking away from this stinking crowd. His head was buzzing from being among all these babbling fuckwits.

He needed some peace and quiet.

And he needed some advice.

There was only one person he could call. The only other person in the world who knew about the tapes and The Visitor. He didn't look forward to talking to that person, because it would mean admitting how stupid he'd been, but he didn't see how he had any choice.

By the time Mark returned to the lobby, most of the witnesses to his moment of embarrassment had moved on. The girl he'd talked to at the front desk was still there, though, and she stared at him. She didn't stop until he got in an elevator and the doors closed in front of him.

EIGHT

AFTER FLEEING SETH MONAHAN'S ROOM, Allison headed in the opposite direction of the elevators. He'd expect that, for one thing. Also, she'd have to deal with the elevator stopping and starting between floors. She didn't want that. Nor did she want anyone who might get on at those other stops to take note of her frazzled demeanor.

In an alcove at the opposite end of the hallway were some vending machines. There was also a door leading to the stairwell. Because she didn't know how long it'd be before Seth realized what she'd done, she eased the door open and shut rather than banging through it. This ran counter to her instincts, but she made herself do it anyway. She'd get through this by being smart and not unthinkingly reactive.

Once she was inside the stairwell and the door was fully shut behind her, she descended at a moderate pace down to the third floor. She didn't run because she didn't want her hurried footsteps echoing in the stairwell, a not inconsiderable factor when one was wearing boots.

The door to the third-floor hallway didn't budge when she tried opening it. She tried again. Same result. She belatedly realized it was only possible to push through stairwell doors from inside the hotel's hallways. There was a card reader on the wall next to the door. Not knowing what else to do, she dug her room card out of a pocket and inserted it in the reader. A second ticked by.

Then the light on the reader changed from red to green.

Thank fuck.

Allison opened the door. Before stepping through it, she glanced back at the flight of stairs leading to the floors above her. She waited a beat and heard nothing. As best she could tell, she was the only person in the stairwell. Seth either remained unaware of what she'd done or was looking for her elsewhere. So far, so good. Letting out a breath, she entered the third-floor hallway and eased the door shut behind her.

Her room was at the far end of the hallway, one of the closest to the elevators. Now that she was no longer so concerned about not being heard, she ran in that direction. The stolen videotape was clutched in her right hand along with her door card. She wished she'd thought to bring her purse with her earlier, but she'd opted to head downstairs with a wad of cash shoved in her pocket instead. Not ordinarily a big deal, but a purse would nicely conceal the tape until she was safely inside her room, at which point she could stash it away in her travel bag. Again, not too big a deal, because she fully expected to be back in her room in a few more seconds.

Choosing haste over care for this final stretch, however, proved costly when the heel of one of her boots snagged on a run in the carpet. Gasping as she pitched forward, the tape and door card flew out of her hand. The tape hit the floor on its side and bounced end over end a few times. A stab of anguish ripped through her as she saw this happen. The feeling intensified when she saw her room card slide under the closed door of a room to her right.

Oh, for fuck's sake.

She pounded a fist against the carpet in frustration.

An overwhelmed part of her psyche wanted to lie here and wallow in her misfortune, but her fear of worse things that might happen if she did that was stronger. She braced her hands on the floor and lurched to her feet.

Retrieving the tape was her first order of business. She staggered over to it and picked it up, allowing herself to lean against the wall as she carefully slid the tape out of its thin cardboard case. Upon closer examination, it was clear the tape was quite old. There were numerous smudges and nicks in the plastic casing. An end of the hand-inked label was curling away from the plastic, the ancient glue losing its adhesive power. The ink itself was smeared nearly to the point of illegibility, but she was able to make out the inscription—*FRIDAY 9 - Homecoming*.

As before, her mind reeled with countless questions.

Where did he get this thing?

How could it possibly exist?

She'd run away from the only person she knew of who might conceivably give her answers, but she wasn't about to go back and start interrogating Seth on the matter. That ship sailed the moment she fled his room. Also, the guy kind of creeped her out and willingly putting herself back in his presence struck her as a horrible idea for all sorts of reasons. Yeah, she wasn't a saint here. She'd taken something that didn't belong to her. Even so, something about him gave her a queasy feeling in her stomach. He might not be full-on psycho, but *something* was off about him.

Outwardly, the tape did not appear damaged. It was surprisingly sturdy for its age. She gave it a careful little shake and listened for anything rattling around inside it. Nothing.

Sighing in relief, she slid the videotape back into its cardboard case and approached room 308. Her room card had gone under this door. She knocked and waited. The door didn't open. Of course not. Nothing could be easy. This was clearly a case of the universe sticking it to her a little for doing something naughty. She put an ear to the door and listened, hearing no sounds of activity, but that didn't necessarily mean anything. There was a DO NOT DISTURB sign on the door handle. Someone might be asleep in there or soaking in the bathtub. Well, too bad for them. She needed that fucking card. The second time she knocked, she did it with the base of her fist, making the door rattle in the frame.

She stepped back and waited.

Once again, nothing happened.

Goddammit.

She dropped down to the floor and pressed a cheek against the carpet as she strained to see under the door. The lights were out in there, but a bit of ambient illumination filtered in through the room's window. She saw the edge of the card on the beige carpet, maybe just a few inches beyond the other side of the door. So close, but probably beyond reach. The gap between the bottom of the door and the carpet was no more than an inch and maybe not even that much. She doubted she'd be able to slide her hand far enough through it to retrieve the card, but she tried anyway, pressing her palm as flat against the floor as she could. Her fingers slid under the door with relative ease, but pushing her knuckles through the gap proved much more difficult. She tried wiggling her hand side to side to wedge it in deeper, but that didn't help much. Her hand was in as far as it would go and the card was still about another inch beyond the tips of her straining fingers.

Fuck.

Before she could retract her hand, another door somewhere nearby opened and someone stepped out into the hallway. Allison turned her head and saw the hairy legs of a heavyset man in cargo shorts and flip-flops.

The man pulled his door shut and moved in her direction, predictably stopping short when he caught sight of her. "Whoa. What's happening here?"

She looked up at him.

He was thirty-ish, maybe slightly older. No flecks of gray yet in his long brown hair, which was gathered up in a man-bun. He had a thick beard and ear gauges and was wearing a black *City of the Living Dead* shirt. Definite con attendee.

Allison grimaced. "Trying to get my fucking door card."

"How did it get under there?"

She told him.

He chuckled, shaking his head ruefully. "Damn. Tough luck."

"Yeah."

He frowned. "Are you checked in under your own name or someone else's?"

"My name."

He shrugged. "Just go down to the front desk and show them an ID. They'll give you another card."

Allison considered telling him her ID was in her wallet, which was in her fucking purse, which she didn't currently have on her fucking person, but she saw no point in extending the conversation. The man couldn't help her in any meaningful way, so the sooner he was out of her hair, the better.

"Thanks. I'll do that."

He dug a phone out of a big hip pocket of his drooping shorts and positioned it above her.

"What are you doing?"

"Exactly what it looks like."

The phone made a shutter-click sound.

"You don't have permission to take my fucking picture, creep."

He chuckled. "Don't need it. Too late anyway." He started moving around her. "Nice ass, by the way."

Allison twisted around, drew a leg back, and kicked out at him, but he narrowly managed to avoid the strike. "Fucker!"

He laughed and continued on toward the elevators.

Seething with anger, Allison extracted her hand from the door gap and got to her feet. The man was waiting at the elevators with his back turned to her, no apparent fear of a second attempt at retaliation. She was so frustrated with everything it was highly tempting to march right up to him and deliver a swift kick to his broad backside, but she clamped down on the impulse, knowing it would only make a bad situation even worse.

The indicator light above one of the elevators showed it was descending from the fifth floor.

Oh, shit.

She turned and ran back down the hallway, ducking into the alcove at the far end to stay out of sight of anyone who might be in that elevator. There was no way to know what Seth was up to at this point, but she was certain he wouldn't remain in his room for long. He'd be looking for her soon, if he wasn't already.

Peering around the corner of the alcove, she saw the elevator open and the people inside it move around to accommodate the man in the cargo shorts. Allison was able to make out some of their faces, but not all of them. She didn't see Seth, but she stayed out of sight until the elevator closed again.

Then she took out her phone and called Cassie.

Her friend answered on the second ring. "A call instead of a text. Something must be wrong."

Allison heaved a breath. "You could say that, yeah. I'm on the third floor. Could you please get up here as fast as fucking possible? I'll explain when you get here."

She was surprised by the hitch in her voice.

And by the tears brimming in her eyes.

This running from danger shit wasn't much fun in real life.

"Hold on, babe, I'll be right there. Don't you go anywhere."

The line went dead.

Allison shivered and whispered a reply only she heard: "I won't."

NINE

FOR THE NEXT TEN MINUTES, Allison stayed hidden in the alcove, her nerves on edge the whole time. She didn't know whether only third floor guests could enter through the stairwell door or any paying guest, but suspected it was the latter, which meant there was a real chance Seth might pop through it at any moment. The prospect was terrifying, but no less so than the chance he might spot her from the elevator should one open on this floor again before she could get into her room. Basically, there was no good option here, so she chose to remain where she was.

A few minutes into her wait, she heard another door open in the hallway, prompting her to glance around the alcove corner again. A teenaged boy who couldn't be more than fourteen or fifteen emerged from a room a few doors down on the right. He wore swim trunks, a sleeveless white T-shirt, and flip-flops, attire that caused her to assume he would head for the elevators and ride down to the ground floor so he could go out to the pool. Instead he headed in her direction.

Allison backed away from the wall corner and moved into position in front of one of the vending machines, pretending to peruse the selection of unhealthy snacks. Without looking at him, she sensed the boy come up behind her as he entered the alcove. He hesitated a moment before approaching the same vending machine. She sensed his awkwardness as he stared for a moment at the snack bags behind the plastic window before glancing at her.

He cleared his throat. "You mind if I go ahead and get something?"

She forced a smile. "Go ahead." She moved aside, giving him room. "I'm having a hard time making up my mind."

The boy fed coins into the slot on the machine, punched in his selection, and waited for the bag to drop down. After retrieving the bag of Fritos, he glanced at her, a frown on his face. "Are you all right?"

Her laugh was as forced as her smile. "I'm fine. Just not having the greatest day." She laughed again when he continued to hesitate. "Seriously. Nothing to worry about here."

He shrugged. "Okay."

The boy walked away from her and a moment later she heard the door to his room close. She let out a breath and again was surprised by a slight welling of tears. It'd been a brief interaction, but the kid was the first person of the male persuasion to treat her decently all day. Hopefully he wouldn't grow up to be a sexist piece of shit.

No other encounters with strangers occurred during the remainder of her wait, a small miracle. The relief she felt when an elevator opened and Cassie stepped out was overwhelming. Her friend's dyed-black hair and perfect Bettie Paige-style bangs were instantly recognizable. She had a towel wrapped around her waist, covering the bottom half of her orange two-piece swimsuit. She wore a white button-down men's shirt over the top half of the suit. The shirt was open in the middle, allowing a view of multiple tattoos and a pierced navel. The strap of a purse was slung over one shoulder.

Allison emerged from her hiding spot and raced toward her friend. A tight embrace right outside the door to their room followed an instant later.

Cassie tried talking to her, but Allison broke out of the embrace and shook her head. "Inside first."

Cassie dug into her purse, searching for her door card.

Allison fidgeted. "Hurry, please."

"Doing my best."

At last, Cassie plucked the card from the depths of her purse and inserted it in the card reader.

Seconds later, they were safely inside the room with the door shut behind them.

Allison set the videotape on the dresser and collapsed onto one of the beds, where she spent some moments sobbing into her hands.

Cassie swept the wet towel away from her waist and allowed it to fall to the floor. She went to the table by the window, dropped her purse on its crowded surface, and settled into one of the chairs there. Choosing to give her friend some time, she took out her phone and spent a couple minutes looking at her various social feeds.

Then she set the phone on the table.

"You're safe now, you know. I won't let anything happen to you."

Allison sat up and took her hands away from her face. She looked at Cassie and smiled. "I know. Thank you. Thanks for coming."

Cassie nodded. "Of course. Now, first things first. Were you attacked? Should I be calling the cops?"

Allison shook her head. "Fuck, no. I'll be lucky if I don't wind up having the cops called on me."

Cassie's expression was inscrutable as she spent a moment studying her friend's face. "Okay," she said at last, shifting slightly in her seat. "Let's hear it. What terrible, heinous thing did you do?"

Allison took a deep breath and proceeded to relay a slightly condensed version of events. Her friend listened without making a sound or interrupting. There was no judgment in her expression, not that Allison expected any. They were ride or die all the way. That was never in doubt. Cassie would help her bury the bodies, if it ever came to that, regardless of the circumstances.

A brief silence ensued when she was done talking.

Cassie appeared deep in thought.

Then she sat up straighter in the chair and leaned forward slightly. "The way I see it, you've got a couple of options here. You can return the tape. That's option number one. I can do it for you, taking someone else along for backup in case the guy actually is dangerous. I'll explain that you acted impulsively and are now regretful. That should be the end of it."

Allison gave an adamant shake of her head. "No."

Cassie nodded. "I figured that'd be your answer after hearing the way you talked about it, but I had to put it on the table on the off-chance you wanted to take the easy way out." She took a deep breath. "So, okay, your other options are as follows. You can stay holed up here in the room the rest of the weekend. It'll be boring as hell, but it's unlikely the guy will be able to track you down. We could stay an extra day, long enough to be sure everyone from the con has cleared out, and then leave. Or you can leave now. There's a side entrance at the bottom of the stairwell. You can go out that way. I'll pull your car around for you and call you when the coast is clear."

Allison's face crinkled with worry. "But what would you guys do? I drove us here. And there's almost two whole days left in the con. I'd hate to ruin your weekend because I did something crazy."

Cassie waved this off. "Don't worry about that. Julia and I will stay. We'll rent a car Monday morning and drive ourselves back. Honestly, I think that's the way to go. You'll be out of harm's way, and we'll hang out here and keep our eyes and ears open, see if we hear anything about this guy looking for you."

Allison shuddered with relief.

Hearing Cassie lay it all out for her calmed her down considerably. She looked at Cassie. "Okay. I want to leave now, as fast as possible. You sure this isn't too much of a hassle?"

"Knock that off. You know it's not."

Allison nodded.

There was a brief silence.

Cassie glanced at the videotape, her gaze lingering on it a moment before shifting back to her friend. "So you really think it's a legit lost *Friday the 13th* movie?"

Allison shrugged. "It sure the fuck looked like it."

Cassie frowned. "Damn. Now you're making me wish we had a VCR up in here."

Allison smiled. "I know. I'd watch it again right this fucking second if we could, but we'll watch it at my place once we're all back home."

"It's a date." Cassie yawned and stretched as she got to her feet. "I'm gonna change into regular clothes and then we'll set this thing in motion. Get your shit packed up. Don't worry about letting Julia know. I'll fill her in later."

Allison nodded. "Okay."

They got busy doing what they needed to do.

TEN

ONCE HE WAS BACK INSIDE his room on the fifth floor, Mark scrolled through the contacts on his phone until he found the entry for his uncle. His index finger hovered above the screen a moment, poised to tap the call button, but he couldn't quite bring himself to initiate the call. Instead he grabbed a beer from the mini fridge and plopped down in a chair near the window.

After pushing some of last night's empties out of the way, he popped the tab on the beer can and took a sip before setting it down again. For the first time, it occurred to him to wonder what the girl must've thought of the shambolic state of his room. Probably figured he'd had a big party in here, but this mess was mostly of his own making. Some girls he met in the bar last night joined him in his room after he invited them up to have drinks and watch vintage horror flicks on VHS. They each had a couple of his beers, but departed after less than an hour, while the *Ilsa, She Wolf of the SS* tape was still playing in the VCR. He still wasn't sure which had offended them more, the movie or his suggestion that they have a threesome.

He turned sullen after they left and started blasting his way through his beer supply, keeping at it until he passed out on the toilet at some point early in the morning. Some hours later, he woke up to discover he'd puked all over himself while unconscious, so it was actually a good thing he'd fallen asleep in a sitting position. Otherwise he might have choked on his vomit like some old school rock and roller.

Mark took another sip of beer and started looking at Twitter on his phone. He searched various hashtags related to the convention and spent quite a while scrolling through photos posted by attendees. Many showed strangers posing with various so-called celebrities booked at the con. While a few genuine genre icons were here this weekend, they were outnumbered by obscure nobodies, people who'd dabbled in acting long ago, appearing in small roles in one or two horror movies in the 80s or 90s before disappearing for decades. Now they were able to make decent coin on the con circuit, posing for pictures with gullible rubes for forty bucks or more a pop. Mark couldn't figure that shit out. The world of fandom was a strange place sometimes.

After about fifteen minutes of rapid scrolling, his breath caught in his throat and his finger froze on the screen.

"There you are, you fucking bitch."

The girl who'd called herself Dana clearly wasn't the focus of the picture. She was in the background, standing at a table in the celebrity room. Other people nearer to the picture-taker were lined up in front of the table to her left. Her body was partly blocked by some old guy standing next to her, but she was leaning forward a bit, allowing for a decent side-profile view of her face. No mistaking that striking visage. Same leather jacket, too. Same platinum blonde hair with black ends. Looking at this image of her now made him feel a little funny, knowing he'd been inside this very same bitch a short while ago.

Some Twitter handles were tagged on the picture and he spent some time looking at those profiles, but as far as he could tell they had no connection to the thief. Same went for the person who'd taken the picture. She just happened to have been in the frame at a fortuitous time. For him, that is.

He saved the picture and cropped it, reducing it to just her face.

He sneered. "I'm gonna find you, bitch. No matter how long it takes, I'm gonna find you. And when I do, God help you."

The relatively quick find motivated him to keep looking a while longer, but he never found another image of his quarry. After an additional half-hour of scrolling, he gave up and accepted that it was time to call his uncle, despite the way the thought made his stomach twist up in tight knots of tension.

He downed the rest of his beer and opened another one.

Then he sat back down, took a deep breath, and made the call.

James Castleberry answered on the third ring. "Yeah?"

The terse answer was standard operating procedure for his uncle. He was a foul-tempered man who lived alone and didn't interact with the world at large unless circumstances compelled it. As a consequence of his aggressively anti-social demeanor, he had no close friends, a trait he shared with his nephew. Mark didn't like his uncle much for a lot of reasons—including vicious beatings he'd received at the man's hands while still a kid. He'd prefer to never have anything to do with the old drunk, but James Castleberry was also the only other person who knew about The Visitor.

Mark cleared his throat. "Uh . . . hi, Uncle James. It's me. Mark."

The man grunted. "I know who the fuck it is. Your name came up on the damn screen. What do you want?"

Mark sighed. "I . . . well, I did something kind of stupid."

His uncle made a throaty sound that was almost a laugh. It was hard to tell, though, because he wasn't a man who laughed a lot. "Of course you did. You're a stupid person. What particular stupid thing have you done now?"

Mark's jaw tightened and his hand clenched on the phone. He really didn't want to have to do this.

But he had no choice.

He cleared his throat again. "I, uh . . ." A heavy sigh. "I lost the *Homecoming* tape."

A pause from the other end.

Mark went on: "The *Friday the 13th* movie. You know, the one our, uh, friend gave me."

"You fucking idiot!" The man screamed the words into his phone, making Mark wince. "Where are you right now?"

Mark grabbed his beer and took a deep slug from the can before answering. "At a horror convention in Virginia."

The man made some guttural sounds that made it clear he was struggling not to erupt in screaming rage again. Sounds that made Mark thankful he was not physically in his uncle's presence at the moment. James Castleberry wasn't quite as tall as his nephew, but he was much more sturdily built, with thick wrists and big hands made for bludgeoning.

"Let me get this straight," he said at last, once he had his anger relatively under control. "You took one of his gifts out of your house, which just that would've been dumb enough, but you also transported it to a location multiple fucking states away."

Mark winced. "That's right."

"Why would you do something so completely fucking stupid?"

Mark delivered the blunt truth for the simple reason that there was no getting around it. "I thought it could get me laid. And it did."

His uncle made more sounds of deep consternation. "You dumb fuck."

Mark sighed. "I know."

He could almost see the man shaking his head at the other end.

"And let me guess. This person you banged . . . wait, was it a chick or a guy?"

Mark frowned. "A girl, of course."

James Castleberry made another of those maybe a laugh/maybe not sounds. "If you say so. This girl, then. She took the tape. After you watched it together. How did she manage that? Were you passed out drunk?"

Mark grimaced. "I was in the shitter."

He spent a few minutes detailing all that had happened since the theft, describing his search for the girl and eventual discovery of her picture on Twitter.

His uncle grunted. "Send me that picture."

Mark put it in a text and hit send.

After the picture went through, James Castleberry made some contemplative sounds as he studied the image. "Unbelievable. You put your life in danger so you could fuck this homely cunt?"

Mark said nothing.

The girl wasn't homely, but there was no use arguing the point. His uncle never missed a chance to belittle or insult him, often in exaggerated ways. This was no exception. Okay, so this "Dana" person wasn't a supermodel or even close, but she was sexy enough in her own right. Otherwise he wouldn't be in this mess.

His uncle sighed. "Kid, you're gonna have to find this girl and get that fucking tape back. Whatever it takes. You know that, right?"

Mark frowned. "Yeah. I know."

James Castleberry's tone shifted to a more somber, less combative tone. "You need to have that tape back in your possession soon. The Visitor's gifts are not to be shared with outsiders. That's the rule. Break that rule and bad things will happen to both of us. I explained all this to you in the beginning. I was very clear about it, wasn't I?"

Again, Mark said nothing.

The man was only telling him what they both already knew.

Mark hadn't treated the rule with the necessary respect. Why? Because he had a hard time fully buying into it. How could The Visitor know when an object as mundane as an old videotape was misplaced or stolen? It'd made no sense to him until the tape was gone. Then he felt its absence like a physical ache, like a malignant sickness devouring him from the inside. Creating a black void only the tape's return could vanquish.

And he felt the shadow of The Visitor on him like a dark cloud.

Following him around.

Watching him.

His uncle made a dismissive sound. "Get your scrawny ass back here as fast as you can. Then we'll get to work finding that bitch. You're not gonna find her there. I can guarantee you she's already gone. But we will fucking track her ugly ass down. And when we're done with her, we'll dump her ass in a landfill. In pieces."

The line went dead.

Mark spent several moments staring blankly at his phone.

Then he finished his beer and grabbed another one from the fridge. He kept at it until all his remaining beers were gone.

Then he went down to the bar.

ELEVEN

TWO DAYS LATER, EARLY MONDAY evening after the convention was over, Mark stood on a median in the parking lot outside the Hyatt, hidden behind the low-hanging branches of a tall tree. An older Mazda convertible with its roof up was parked with its back end against the curb. The tree's long branches extended outward over the back half of the car, shading much of its interior from the worst of the summer heat, though Mark doubted shade was a factor in the driver choosing this parking location. In that case, it would've made far more sense to park with the front end against the curb. Then again, as he'd learned over the years, the decisions girls made often made no sense.

The Mazda was owned by Tina the desk clerk. She'd parked it in this same spot the last two days. The median was at the far reaches of the hotel's large parking area. On the other side of the median was a narrow access road that led to a city street. Mark wasn't sure why the girl would choose to park so far away from the hotel itself. There must be some closer area designated for employee parking. Maybe she enjoyed the long walk. Seemed stupid to Mark, but it was just one more thing to attribute to the disorganized nature of the female mind.

Mark checked the time on his phone. It was right around the same time he'd observed her leaving the hotel last night. Sure enough, before long he spied her threading her way through cars in the parking sections closer to the Hyatt. Just like last night, her head was down and her attention on the phone gripped in her right hand. Her dark brown hair was hanging in her face, yet another thing impairing situational awareness. His estimation of her intelligence kept plummeting downward, though in fairness it'd never been high. It was weird. Weren't chicks usually on high alert in situations like this? Perhaps she was one of the rare lucky ones who'd never been accosted by random predatory weirdos in public places. He could think of no other plausible reason for her nonchalance.

Hiding behind the tree probably wasn't even necessary, but he did it anyway, just to be extra sure she wouldn't spot him before reaching her car. She glanced up one time as she neared the Mazda, but only long enough to confirm her trajectory. She didn't put the phone away until she arrived at the vehicle's driver side door, dropping it in her large handbag at the same moment she hit the unlock button on her key fob. When the car made its high-pitched unlocking sound, Mark emerged from behind the tree and swiftly rushed up behind her, slapping a hand over her mouth and placing the edge of the butcher knife against the tender flesh of her throat.

She squirmed in his grasp, but he easily held her in place. "Don't scream or I'll slit your throat."

She whimpered, muffled sounds of begging emerging from behind his hand. He laughed and let go of her, spinning her around so she could see him.

Her face was wet with tears and she was trembling as she stared confusedly at him. "Please don't hurt me."

He laughed again. "I'm not gonna hurt you, for fuck's sake. I was just giving you a good scare. Let this be a lesson. You should pay more attention to your surroundings."

He removed the Michael Myers mask from his head.

Her brow furrowed. "It's you."

Mark smirked. "Yes, it's me, the object of your desire. Aren't you happy to see me?"

She pouted as she wiped her tears away. "You scared the shit out of me, asshole. I really thought I was about to die."

"Come on, I'm harmless. I was just trying to give you a good scare."

She grunted. "Well, you did a real bang-up job of that. So congratulations. I guess." She eyed him up and down, still pouting. "What's up with the jumpsuit? Are you a janitor or something?"

Mark laughed. "Hell, no. Do I look like I'd have a loser job like that? This is my Michael Myers costume."

She crossed her arms, blew the hair out of her face, and leaned back against the Mazda. She seemed calmer now. That was good. He figured she was still interested in him despite the scare he'd given her—and despite having seen him make a fool of himself in the lobby Saturday afternoon. Otherwise she'd be getting in her car right now and trying to get as far away from him as fast as she could.

"Who the fuck is Michael Myers?"

Now it was his turn to frown. "Seriously? You don't know who Michael Myers is? How is that possible?"

She rolled her eyes. "Not everyone is a horror nerd."

"But everybody knows Michael Myers. And Freddy. And Jason. Don't they?"

She shook her head. "No, Mark. They don't. Also, the stupid convention is over. If you wanted to see me again, there were probably better ways to go about it than jumping out at me in a fucking Michael Myers costume." She frowned. "Wait. This *is* about wanting to see me again, isn't it?"

He showed her his most sheepish and disarming smile, a look he'd practiced to perfection over the years. "Of course. I would've tried sooner, but I wasn't sure you'd give me the time of day after that scene in the lobby. I'm leaving in the morning tomorrow, though, and figured I had to take one last shot."

They stared silently at each other a moment.

Then she sighed. "So where are you going when you leave here?"

Mark's smile gave way to a regretful grimace. "Back home to Illinois."

She frowned. "That's so far away."

He nodded. "I know."

"We might never see each other again."

His turn to sigh. "Yeah. Sucks, huh?"

Her head turned toward the hotel and she stared silently in that direction for a few moments. He guessed she wasn't really looking at anything in particular. She was having an internal debate about something and didn't want to make eye contact with him while it was in process.

She looked at him. "Get in the car."

She opened the driver side door and slipped in behind the wheel without waiting for him to reply.

Suppressing a smirk, Mark went around to the other side, opened the door there, and dropped into the passenger seat. The first thing he noticed about the Mazda's interior was how immaculately clean it was. Not a speck of dirt or a smudge anywhere. It made him think she'd paid for it with her own money. If it'd been a family hand-me-down, she probably wouldn't have been quite so devoted to keeping it spotless. He set the Michael Myers mask up on the dashboard, mashing it up against the window so it wouldn't slip and slide during the drive. The butcher knife went into the door pocket on his side.

Tina started the car and drove out of the parking space. She put her headlights on. It wasn't full dark yet, but the light was beginning to drain from the sky. Once they were out on the access road, she hit the gas and the engine revved as they raced along the curving lane. She stepped on the brake, bringing the Mazda to a squealing stop at a red light a half-mile later.

He glanced at her, smiling. "Wow, you're a real . . ." He trailed off a moment, unable to think of a famous race car driver. "Daredevil. You're a real daredevil."

She looked at him and smirked. "In more ways than one, Mr. Myers." She reached over and gave his crotch a squeeze, making him gulp. "As you're about to find out."

Her hand came away from his crotch when the light turned green. She hit the gas again and the tires squealed as she blew through the intersection. A fast spin of the wheel took them on a leftward trajectory. Once the car was pointed straight down the road again, she put the gas pedal to the floor and they took off like a rocket, the engine roaring. She soon took them out of the main part of town and out into the dark countryside. By then it was even darker and she put on high beams as she sped along swooping and plunging back roads unlit by street lamps. He braced his feet against the footwell, grabbed the handle over his head, and held on for dear life.

Mark didn't know this area and had no sense of where they were or where they were going, except that after several minutes of this they seemed to be climbing to a higher elevation. Shortly after the ground finally leveled out, she took them down a relatively straight stretch of road. After about another half-mile, it curved slightly and there was a place up on the right where there was a break in the trees shrouding the right-hand side of the road. She slowed the Mazda and pulled into that spot, which turned out to be a scenic bluff overlooking the town. There was a fence at the edge of the bluff and beyond it he could see the twinkling downtown lights off in the distance.

She put the car in park, revved the engine one more time for the hell of it, and cut it off, leaving the key turned far enough forward to lower the windows. After that, she popped her seatbelt off and turned toward him, indicating the view with a tilt of her head. "So? What do you think?"

Mark glanced out at the twinkling lights again for a moment.

Then he looked at her. "It's, uh . . . nice. Very romantic."

She leaned toward him, an openly lustful expression on her face. "Speaking of romance . . ."

She bit his bottom lip, then slid her tongue into his mouth.

"Oomph."

Mark kissed her back even as he groped blindly for the seat buckle. After some moments of futility, she unbuckled it for him. Then she took her tongue out of his mouth and bit his lip again.

"Ouch."

She laughed and grabbed his zipper tab, tugging it down as she shifted in her seat. In another moment, her head was in his lap. She freed his erection from his underpants and took it into her mouth.

Mark gasped.

He gulped and swallowed with difficulty.

"Wow. Jesus. You really get down to it in a hurry, don't you?"

She made a muffled sound that might have been a noise of affirmation.

Mark was stunned.

He'd bedded some horny babes in his time, but this marked a new standard in seduction speed, one he seriously doubted could ever be bested. Hell, it barely counted as seduction. He could only surmise she was trying extra hard to impress him for reasons of her own.

In that case, mission fucking accomplished.

She made loud slurping noises as her head went rapidly up and down like a piston, her tongue doing things that made his toes curl. Her technique was incredible, unquestionably the best he'd ever experienced.

As she continued to work at him, he leaned forward slightly and reached toward the dashboard. She made a noise of angry protest and pushed him back against the seat. He acquiesced for a few moments, but then quickly leaned forward and snatched the mask off the dashboard, pulling it on over his head as he leaned back against the seat.

Then he allowed himself to relax and resumed enjoying what she was doing. Things built to a head—*haha*—in fairly short order after that, as his ejaculate erupted inside her mouth less than a minute later.

After she was done sucking him dry, she sat up and twisted around in her seat again, leaning out the window to spit out his load. She spat a couple times. Then she settled back into her seat and, after wiping her mouth with the back of a hand, turned to look at him with a smile on her face.

The smile faded. "Why did you put that thing back on?"

He made exaggerated heavy breathing sounds.

Tina rolled her eyes. "Cute. You do kind of sound like he does in the movies. Myers, I mean."

Mark tilted his head. "You fucking liar. You *have* heard of Michael Myers."

She laughed. "Of course I have. Everybody knows who he is. Even people who aren't horror nerds. I was just fucking with you earlier." Another laugh. "Revenge for scaring me like that."

Mark resumed the heavy breathing.

Tina snorted. "It's not gonna work this time. Not after I've had your dick in my mouth."

Mark retrieved the butcher knife from the door pocket and showed it to her. Moonlight shining in through the windshield glinted off the blade.

She shook her head. "Nope. Still not scary."

Mark grunted. "I was wondering if you could do me a favor."

She arched an eyebrow. "What kind of favor?"

"I want you to go into your computer at work and get me a list of all the guests at the hotel this weekend. Their names and all the information on file for them. Addresses and such. I'm particularly interested in female guests."

Her smile vanished. "That's a joke, right?"

"No."

She frowned. "I can't do that. You're hot and all, but no way in hell will I risk losing my job for you."

Mark stared at her for an extended silent moment.

Then he nodded.

"That's too bad, but it's what I figured you'd say."

He started in with the heavy breathing again.

She reached for the key in the ignition slot. "Fuck this. I thought we could hang out and talk a while, but I'm taking you back. You're being way too weird."

Mark leaned over and shoved her back against the seat before she could start the car. He rammed the big blade into her abdomen. She screamed as warm blood touched his fingers. The sound was louder than he expected, like a fucking air raid siren going off right in his ear. It went on and on. Amazingly, the volume went up even higher when he twisted the knife in her gut. She clawed at his face, but couldn't scratch him because of the mask. He pulled the knife out and jammed it in again, liking the way her weak flesh yielded to the strength of steel. Many times he'd imagined how this might feel, but the reality was so much better. She tried twisting away from him, clawing at the door handle with a shaking hand, but he held her in place. As he watched her cry and plead, he thought about the girl who'd stolen his tape and imagined he was doing this to her instead of boring old Tina.

He took the knife out of her gut and jabbed the blade into her neck. She gagged on the steel in her throat. When he removed it, a crazy spray of blood arced outward, spattering the steering wheel, dashboard, and windshield. Soon her eyes started to glaze over, her head lolling forward.

Mark knew she was dead when the blood flow ceased.

After drinking in the sight of her lifeless form a moment longer, he got out of the car and went around to the other side, where he opened the door and hauled out her body. He took hold of her wrists and dragged her into the nearby stand of trees, far enough to ensure she wouldn't be easily spotted by a passerby even in daytime.

Then he returned to the car, adjusted the front seat to accommodate his longer, lankier frame, and settled in behind the wheel, reveling in the stickiness of the blood beneath him. He glanced at himself in the rearview mirror and smiled behind the mask.

He felt better now. Stronger.

Capable of doing all the things he'd have to do to get that tape back and have his revenge. He removed the mask and dropped it on the passenger seat. After that, he took out his phone. He was unsurprised to see another barrage of angry messages from James Castleberry. There was a man who didn't like being disobeyed or ignored.

To understate.

Mark pulled up his GPS app, entered an address near the Hyatt, and started the car.

TWELVE

HER DEPARTURE FROM THE HYATT was stressful, despite never once catching sight of the guy calling himself Seth. They orchestrated things exactly as Cassie proposed. Down the stairs to the side entrance, with Allison waiting behind the door while her friend retrieved her car. The trip down the stairs was okay, with Cassie accompanying her. As soon as she was left alone, however, her nerves were on edge. Paranoia consumed her. She did a lot of pacing around in the little area inside the door, biting her nails and throwing lots of anxious glances up the stairs.

Only around ten minutes passed while she was left alone there, but it felt more like ten hours. The door was plate glass. She tried her best to stay away from it on the off-chance Seth happened to walk by, as unlikely as that seemed. There wasn't a lot of foot traffic in the area outside the door, as it wasn't a convenient point of entry for anyone who hadn't lucked into a parking space right at the sidewalk. Her thoughts in those moments, however, were not driven by things like logic or probability odds. Instead, she was a slave to fear.

She tried countering fear by reminding herself she knew nothing about Seth. Something about him set off internal warning bells, but there was no tangible proof he was actually psychotic or otherwise unstable. He'd demonstrated no overt tendencies in that area, but that meant little due to the brevity of their time together. She also had no idea whether he was actively trying to chase her down. That was just an assumption on her part. It might be the truth, but she didn't *know* that. For all she knew, he'd shrugged it off as an unfortunate consequence of hooking up with a stranger. It was at least remotely possible he'd be relatively chill about it if they somehow happened to bump into each other.

Allison tried hard to make herself believe in those more benign possibilities, but she wasn't buying any of it. If she'd impulsively swiped some commonplace item, maybe it wouldn't be a big deal, but this wasn't any ordinary theft. She'd done a Google search on the movie's title while still up in the room with Cassie. Not one reference to it showed up anywhere. Even if *Homecoming* was simply an extraordinarily upscale fan film, there should be something about it out there, but no matter what search terms she used, she turned up absolutely zilch. This only added fuel to her paranoia, confirming her suspicion that the tape she'd taken was something rare and special. Losing something like that wasn't something a person could just take in stride.

He was looking for her.

And he was angry as hell.

She had absolutely no doubt on either count. Even worse, she couldn't blame him one damn bit. In his place, she'd be furious—and determined to get the movie back by any means necessary.

Allison nearly jumped out of her skin when her phone vibrated in her jacket pocket. She took it out and looked at the screen.

Cassie.

She answered the call and put the phone to her ear. "Hey."

"I'm here."

Inside of a minute later, after accepting a quick hug from Cassie, she was behind the wheel of her 2019 Chevrolet Cruze. She tossed her travel bag in the back and set her GPS for the trip home. After exchanging some hurried parting words with her friend, she drove away from the Hyatt.

Her paranoia lingered even after the hotel disappeared from view. She had less than half a tank of gas but elected not to fill up until after she left the town behind. What she had would take her a decent distance down the road. Better to put some serious miles between herself and this place than risk any chance of running into Seth at a local gas station, regardless of how minimal that risk might be.

She didn't start relaxing until she was nearly a hundred miles down the highway. At that point, she did finally pull off at an exit and gas up the Cruze. She took the time to call Cassie for a brief chat. After that, she got right back on the road and focused on driving, keeping the music off and listening only to the sound of her GPS app's voice navigator and the hum of her tires on asphalt. She wanted no distractions, nothing other than her own thoughts cluttering her mind as she drove with precision and speed. The journey back to her home in Hilliard—a suburb of Columbus—took right around eight hours.

The lingering paranoia still with her during the drive eased somewhat once she was back inside her little house, but it did not vanish entirely. After shrugging off her jacket and depositing her travel bag on her bed, she did a full circuit of the house, checking to be sure every door and window was locked up tight. She put on all the exterior lights and set the alarm.

Only then did she begin to feel how weary she was from the hours of driving and anxiety. She got out of her clothes and took a hot shower, luxuriating in the soothing spray for a long while. After drying off and changing into comfier clothes, she figured she'd soon crawl into bed and either take a nap or sleep through the night. The hour was an early one for her, but so what? She was tired and this hadn't been a normal day in so many ways. Shutting off her mind and allowing herself a long period of rejuvenation was unquestionably the smart thing to do.

With that in mind, she stripped off her Camp Crystal Lake sweatpants and crawled into bed.

She was so tired she neglected to turn off her bedside lamp before sleep overtook her.

Allison awoke with a start and sat up panting, her heart racing as images from the terrifying dream lingered. In the dream, a shadowy figure had pursued her through her house. Only her house seemed much larger than it really was, with more hallways and rooms. She walked fast through the bewildering maze of the house, knowing something was behind her. Something that was getting closer by the moment. She felt cold, freezing air on the back of her neck and then her whole body felt rimed with frost. The thing behind her wasn't human, though how she knew that was impossible to say, because she was too terrified to glance backward.

Until right at the end of the dream.

In the last moment before she woke up, she turned her head and saw the slender shape of a man with a face like melting wax. He wore a long black coat and a black hat with a wide brim tilted low over his blurry face. His mouth was a lipless oval, a shape that shifted and became a black circle. No words emerged, but in some unknown way something was communicated anyway. The man with the melting face had something to do with the videotape. She couldn't possess it without giving herself to him. Her pace through the hallway turned maddeningly slow. This wasn't by choice. She willed herself to go faster, but she could not. It was like trying to run underwater.

Then she felt the melting man's cold hand on her shoulder.

And that's when she woke up, with a scream on her lips.

Still shaking, she leaned over and checked her phone, which was on the little bedside table. Not even five in the morning yet, well before her normal up for the day time, but she had no desire to go back to sleep. She rarely had recurring dreams, but even a slight risk of encountering that strange figure again was something she wanted to avoid.

Allison got up and went into the kitchen to put on a pot of coffee.

THIRTEEN

CASSIE CAME OVER TUESDAY NIGHT.

They had a brief conversation earlier in the day, during which her friend told her to expect a full report on the remainder of the con, teasing Allison with hints of Seth sightings. She also made it clear she expected a viewing of the purported lost *Friday* sequel.

Allison spent part of the afternoon cleaning up the place. This didn't take an inordinate amount of time. Her place was often cluttered, but it was never filthy. Despite loving animals, she owned no pets, so it was easy to maintain a basic level of cleanliness at all times. Once she was satisfied with the state of the place, she went out to a nearby beverage store and bought two bottles of red wine and two six-packs of expensive beer. She considered getting food from the grocery store, but decided they'd have something delivered. Not being much of a cook herself, having little kitchen proficiency beyond the most basic things, this was probably the better option anyway.

The doorbell rang at six o'clock.

Allison went to the front door and took a look through the peephole. Cassie stood alone on the porch, her eyes hidden by dark sunglasses shaped to look like bat wings. She was wearing a short black dress with white polka dots. Standard attire for her far more fashion-conscious friend, whereas Allison had donned black shorts and yet another of her many *Friday the 13th* shirts, this one displaying an image of Jason Voorhees standing beneath a full moon with a bloody machete in his hand.

She opened the door.

Cassie smiled. "Hey."

"Hey."

Cassie had arrived bearing a six-pack of the same brand of craft beer Allison had purchased earlier. If nothing else, they were unlikely to run out of booze tonight, unless they got carried away and went on a mini-bender. Though that wasn't a common occurrence for them, it wasn't exactly unprecedented either.

Allison moved aside with her hand still on the doorknob, allowing Cassie room enough to come into the foyer. She then closed the door and locked it up tight. Standard bottom lock, deadbolt, and chain lock. These were the locks that were already in place when she bought the house. Until lately, they'd made her feel reasonably secure, but now she was wondering whether it might be a good idea to upgrade to state-of-the-art stuff. Though she'd calmed down some since Saturday, she was still a bit on edge. That guy was out there somewhere, maybe actively trying to track her down. She still wasn't sure how serious a threat he might be, but pretending the possibility of being stalked didn't exist would be foolish. Then there was the matter of her dreams about the mysterious figure.

The man with the melting face.

He'd come after her again multiple times. Every time she slept, so far. It was becoming stressful. This was her first episode of recurring nightmares in pretty much her entire life and she didn't like it one bit. She assumed the figure represented her anxiety about everything that had transpired since Saturday, just an admittedly creepy symbol, but this hypothesis did little to ease the dread the dreams instilled in her.

They went into the kitchen and Cassie stashed the six-pack in the fridge, chuckling when she saw the identical sixers that were already in there. She took out two brown bottles and bumped the fridge door shut with her hip. "We're all set up for a little party, looks like."

Allison took the bottles from her and popped off the caps with an opener designed to look like the weed whacker Jason Voorhees used as a murder weapon in *The New Blood*. She handed a bottle to Cassie. They clinked bottles and took a drink.

"Cheers," Cassie said.

They went out the back door to the little deck that overlooked

Allison's small backyard. There were lounge chairs, but they opted to sit at the umbrella-shaded deck table.

Allison took another sip of beer. "I figured we'd just order something. Pizza or Chinese. Whatever you want."

"Let's do pizza."

"Fine by me."

Allison placed the order with an app on her phone.

She set the phone on the table and leaned back in her chair. "So, let's hear it. How did the rest of the con go?"

Cassie set her sunglasses on the table and shifted slightly in the chair, crossing her legs. "I spent a lot of time keeping an eye out for your man."

Allison grimaced. "Ugh. Don't call him that."

Cassie laughed. "What should I call him then?"

"I don't know. Just not that."

Cassie sighed. "Fine. His name's Seth, right? I'll call him that."

Allison's expression darkened and she chewed her bottom lip in a worried way.

Cassie eyed her curiously. "What's wrong?"

Allison shrugged. "I don't think that's his real name. I think the ID he showed me was a really good fake. Plugged the license number into some places online and it kept coming back as invalid. Did some more digging around and couldn't find any reference to a Seth Monahan living in Lafayette, Indiana."

Cassie frowned. "Huh. That's some shady shit."

"Yep."

Cassie looked off toward the sound of a barking dog somewhere else in the neighborhood, appearing to think about something. She took a big gulp of beer before sighing and looking at Allison. "That bugs me. I don't know if it's actually scary, but it doesn't sit well. I get why you gave him a phony name. That was a safety thing. But this guy had no reason to fear you. So why does he show you a fake ID right off the fucking bat?"

"I really don't know."

Hearing the troubled tone in her friend's voice, Cassie reached over and touched the back of Allison's hand. "Hey, it's okay. The guy knows nothing about you. He has no way of finding you. You're *safe*. Got it?"

Allison blinked moisture from her eyes and nodded. "Yeah. I got it."

I think.

I hope.

Cassie picked up her beer bottle and leaned back again. "I would suggest you take down all your social media, at least for a while. Take down or hide anything you can that points to you."

Allison nodded. "Already done. I need a break from all that shit anyway."

Cassie smiled. "Good girl. So, I kept an eye out for this guy, and I did wind up spotting him several times over the next couple days."

"You didn't try to talk to him, did you?"

Cassie made a face and shook her head. "God, no. And I didn't need to go looking for him, either. He was around a lot, sort of patrolling all the main rooms over and over. He radiated agitation. You could tell he was looking for something or somebody."

Allison frowned. "Me. He was looking for me."

Cassie sighed. "I'd like to suggest otherwise, but yeah, probably so."

Allison took a big gulp of beer. "Let's not talk about him for a while. Were you guys able to have any actual fun, or did I ruin the whole weekend?"

"Stop. You didn't ruin anything." Cassie's tone was playful, but adamant. She held Allison's gaze long enough to drive the point home. "I'm serious. You didn't. Understand?"

"If you say so. But did you? Have any fun, I mean?"

Cassie smirked. "Oh, yeah. I kept an eye out for you-know-who during the day, but at night we played. Drinking. Karaoke. The usual con shenanigans." She chuckled. "And you weren't the only one who got some action."

Allison raised an eyebrow. "You hooked up with somebody?"

Cassie shook her head. "Not me. Julia. She and some guy she met in the dealer room hit it off. One of the vendors. He hung out with us all night Saturday, even went to the midnight screening of *Night of the Demons* with us. They were all over each other and left not even halfway through. Didn't see her again until late the next morning."

A sense of crawling unease made Allison shiver. "Hmm."

"I can see what you're thinking. I got no bad vibes from this guy. Wouldn't have let her go off with him otherwise." Cassie chuckled again. "Did make me a little jealous, though. Of him."

Allison laughed.

They talked about other things for a while. Allison grabbed more beers from the fridge while Cassie spent a few minutes in the bathroom. The pizza arrived and they had some hot slices with their beers out on the deck. By then both were experiencing the first mild tinglings of a buzz.

It was time for the main event.

Allison opened one of the wine bottles and carried it into the living room along with a couple glasses. She poured a glass for each of them before disappearing into her bedroom for a few minutes. When she returned, it was with the purloined videotape in hand.

Cassie's eyes widened with interest. She sat at one end of Allison's plush black sofa, with her bare feet tucked beneath her. "Ooh, is that it?"

"Yep."

The living room was outfitted with two televisions. A 60-inch 4K flatscreen was mounted to the wall. Beneath that was a large vintage floor model Zenith. Atop the Zenith was a top-loading Panasonic VCR. Each of the obsolete pieces of technology dated from the early 80s and were in excellent working order. When buying vintage items, Allison always procured the best-maintained ones she could find, even if it meant paying more. She loaded the tape in the VCR, grabbed the remote, and joined her friend on the sofa.

"Have you watched it again since you got back?"

Allison picked up her wine glass and took a sip. "You know I fucking did."

Cassie laughed softly, a note of mild self-deprecation in the sound. "Yeah, dumb question. Here's a better one. How many times have you seen it now?"

"This will be the fourth time."

Cassie tilted her head, eyeing her quizzically. "Fourth time since getting home or . . ."

"Fourth time altogether."

Including that time with the creepy dude.

This was mutually understood, but went unspoken.

Allison aimed the remote at the VCR and hit the play button. She felt her friend's gaze linger on her a moment longer, monitoring her for signs of distress. That stopped shortly after the promo montage began playing on the Zenith's screen.

Cassie's early reactions to what she was seeing were mostly varying shades of amusement. As Allison suspected would happen, that changed when she saw the dual decapitation scene at the boat dock, when she let out the first of several astonished gasps that came in quick succession over the next few minutes.

She looked at Allison as the opening credits sequence came to an end. "Oh my God."

Allison couldn't help smiling. "Yeah."

Hearing her friend's amazed reactions, especially at this early stage of watching the movie, was taking some of the edge off her anxiety. She was feeling lighter of spirit and on the verge of having something actually resembling a good time. Of course, the booze was helping, too, loosening her up and allowing her to forget all about the man with the melting face for a while.

"That was Ryan fucking Laettner."

Allison laughed. "Yep."

Cassie shook her head as her gaze returned to the screen. "Holy shit."

These excited exclamations recurred at various points throughout the film, but the time gaps between them lengthened as Cassie became inexorably more entranced by what was happening on the screen. Allison watched her face nearly as much as she watched the movie. The feelings playing out there closely matched what she'd felt seeing it the first time. An almost perfect mirror. More astonished gasps came as the film's hyper-violent concluding sequences unfolded. The final shocking shot right before the credits rolled made her jump, causing a small bit of red wine to slosh over the rim of her glass. She barely noticed as the droplets touched the fabric of her dress. By then they'd polished off the first bottle of wine and started on the second. They were no longer just mildly buzzed, but were not yet smashed.

Allison set her glass down and lowered the volume as the credits continued to roll.

Cassie looked at her. "That is not a fucking fan film."

Allison nodded. "No. It's not."

The look on Cassie's face shifted and conveyed varying things over the next few moments, but overriding all of it was a state of deep puzzlement. "That's a real *Friday the 13th* sequel. From a long time ago. And it looks like it was shown on fucking HBO."

Another nod from Allison. "I know."

She'd already been through the same stages of disbelief, confusion, and inevitable acceptance of what was right in front of her eyes, regardless of how impossible it seemed.

Cassie grunted. "I don't understand. How can this be?"

Allison gulped down the last of the wine in her glass and filled it again. She shifted around on the sofa and looked Cassie in the eye. "It can't. It's not possible. Not in this world."

Cassie frowned. "What are you saying?"

Allison hesitated briefly.

Then she took a deep breath and dove in. "Okay, so this is going to sound crazy, but I've thought about it and thought about it, and I can't come up with anything else that makes sense. It's not a fan film. We're already in agreement there. And we know that the actual ninth installment in the *Friday* franchise was *Jason Goes to Hell*. It was the first in the series to be distributed by New Line rather than Paramount. This is established, undeniable fact. And yet we just watched a movie called *Friday the 13th Part IX: Homecoming*. It appears to have been distributed by Paramount. It can't be a lost sequel. That was my original theory, but it makes no sense. Word of it would've leaked out. Therefore, it makes no rational sense that this movie exists. Like I said, not in this world." She paused to take another breath. "So there's just one reasonable conclusion. *Homecoming* isn't from this world."

Cassie stared at her in silence for an extended time. There was no disbelief in her expression. Nor did she look like a person attempting to hide a feeling that her best friend had lost her mind. Instead, she was in a state of deep thought. Her gaze flicked to the television screen and back again.

"Where is it from then?"

Allison sipped wine. "Imagine an alternate reality. A different timeline. Maybe there's a bunch of different ones. We've seen this shit in movies, but what if it's a real thing? What if this movie comes from one of those different timelines? A place where everything is exactly the same as here . . . up to a point. Things diverge, take different paths. Then we have alternate histories. Maybe in some of those timelines COVID-19 never fucking happened. Maybe a game show host never became president. And maybe there are movies we've never seen here."

Cassie shook her head. "Hmm. Let's say you're right. I don't know if I totally buy the theory yet, because it's quite a fucking leap, but for the sake of argument, we'll go with it. So it's from another world. Fine. But how did it get to this world? And how did that jerk at the con wind up with it?"

This is where Allison's theories hit a dead end.

She groaned and shook her head. She stared into the wine in her glass and frowned. "I don't fucking know, goddammit."

Cassie leaned over and touched her arm. "Are you okay?"

Tears bloomed in Allison's eyes. "No. Not even close. And I've been having nightmares. Really, really bad ones about a man with a melting face. He has something to do with the tape. He chases me. He . . . he . . ."

Cassie squeezed her arm. "Do you want me to stay the night?"

Allison sniffled. "Will you? I'd love that."

Cassie smiled. "Of course." She reached for the wine bottle. "Now let's get busy drinking up the rest of the booze in this house."

Allison had a massive hangover when she woke up the next morning, the likes of which she hadn't experienced in quite some time. This was no mild headache or quickly passing bout of nausea. Her stomach was tied up in knots and her head felt like it was being crushed by a steel band. It took her a while to realize Cassie was already gone.

And even longer to realize the tape was gone, too.

FOURTEEN

IN THE TIME SINCE HIS departure from Virginia, Mark Castleberry hadn't experienced anything even faintly reminiscent of a moment's peace. The rush that came with killing the hotel clerk began to fade within minutes of fleeing the kill scene in the dead girl's car.

The murder was precipitated by an unbearable level of pent-up tension, a feeling primarily driven by fear of what his uncle would do once he returned home, as well as fear of The Visitor. The latter was an unknown quantity. His uncle said there would be severe consequences for losing one of The Visitor's gifts. Mark believed him, but he had no clue what form those consequences might take. He could only worry so much about the unknowable. His uncle was another story. He already knew all-too-well how that man's considerable wrath would manifest itself.

Because his fear of the man was so intense, he was reluctant to return home at all. He knew he would have to eventually, but he was so uptight about it, the worry felt like it was burning a hole in his stomach. The situation wasn't helped any by the extreme level of paranoia gripping him every step of the way on the journey back to Illinois. Wherever he went, he kept expecting a swarm of cops to materialize out of nowhere and take him down. He had a hard time looking TSA agents in the eye at the airport. Once he was on the plane, he fidgeted nonstop, always looking around for the sky marshall he was sure would soon take him off the plane and off to jail. He became convinced anyone he caught staring at him a moment too long was an undercover officer, even the bitches he'd normally suspect were drooling over him.

The fear of imminent apprehension continued even after he was on the ground in Illinois. He retrieved his car from the parking garage, expecting to feel relief once he was back inside its familiar confines, but that did not happen. Instead, he spent the drive back toward his hometown shaking behind the wheel and constantly checking the rearview for signs of pursuit by law enforcement.

On top of all that, his conscience was doing a number on him. The biggest surprise in that area, of course, was finding he still had some semblance of one. He kept thinking about the girl in Virginia not being alive anymore. He'd killed her to vent his rage at another girl entirely. She hadn't deserved it. And almost right up to the moment he went through with it, a part of him persisted in believing he wasn't the kind of person who could do something like that. Obviously he'd been wrong, but the surprising thing was how much he hated it. He'd never been any kind of saint, but he hadn't thought he was an actual bad person until then. So now it was eating him up inside, the way he couldn't stop thinking of her family and what it would do to them when her body was discovered.

This led to gloomy thoughts of self-sacrifice.

I should turn myself in.

No, I should kill myself.

The prospect of jail made him think of every movie or TV show he'd ever seen that was set in prison. It didn't take long to decide the notion of spending years or decades behind bars was unacceptable. He deserved punishment, but he wouldn't be able to survive for long in an environment like that. He didn't want to get shivved in the showers or turned into somebody's bitch. The lack of freedom wouldn't be much fun either.

Suicide wasn't a terribly attractive option either, but at least it'd be over fast, if he did it right. The only thing holding him back was his lack of certainty about what—if anything—came after death. He didn't want to burn in the fires of hell for all eternity for his misdeed, nor was he too thrilled about the possibility of simply ceasing to exist altogether.

He was overwhelmed and needed time to think.

So instead of returning to his house that first night back, he checked into a motel a little outside his hometown. After checking in, he walked to a gas station across the street, where he loaded up on snacks and a case of Budweiser in cans. He was so lost in thought as he came back across the street that he didn't notice his uncle's blue work van parked next to his own Mustang until he was almost right up to the space between the vehicles.

A door on the van swung open and out stepped his uncle.

James Castleberry looked angry.

Angrier than Mark had ever seen him, in fact, which was saying a lot. His legs turned rubbery and the plastic bags clutched in his hands felt on the verge of sliding from his fingers. A whimper nearly escaped his lips, but he was able to stifle it at the last moment. "Uncle James. What are you doing here?"

James Castleberry sneered as he came closer. "What you mean is, how did I find you? Right?"

Mark said nothing.

The older man looked like he'd been working on his cars all day. He had a lot, many of them vintage muscle cars, and he spent a lot of his time tinkering with them. His jeans were filthy, smeared with grease and other things. The same went for the denim button-up shirt he wore open over a faded Molly Hatchet T-shirt. Old jailhouse tattoos were visible on his forearms, along with a number of scars. He was balding up top, but he had a handlebar mustache and long hair in the back. And then there was the ever-present Confederate battle flag symbol on his belt buckle. Once, when he was a kid, Mark made fun of that belt buckle.

He never did that again.

His uncle looked him up and down, making a sound of disgust as he shook his head. "You look like you're about to piss your pants, you big sissy. Tracking you down was easy. When you stopped responding to my messages, I figured you might pull a disappearing act, so I went out to the airport and hunted around until I found your car. I put a GPS tracker on it, and now here we are."

Mark felt close to hyperventilating.

He considered dropping the things he'd purchased and running off. There was a wooded area behind the motel. He could run deep into the woods and hide out there for a while, maybe long enough for his uncle to get tired of waiting for him to reemerge. Hopefully he'd go away and wait to settle things with him another time.

But the look on the man's face told him that would never happen.

By grudging mutual agreement, they went into the room Mark had rented. It was one of those weekly stay places, so he'd paid for it through the following Sunday. As Mark set his purchases on the table, his uncle closed and locked the door, then closed the curtains. Now the only illumination was courtesy of the bedside lamp, which was fitted with a weak bulb. His uncle looked even more monstrous than usual in the semi-gloom, like a predatory, primordial beast that lived in shadows. Now here he was in the shadows with him, drawn helplessly into a trap from which he could not escape.

James Castleberry cracked the knuckles of his right hand, a loud popping sound that made his nephew wince. "I told you to come home right away. Remember that? Saturday, that was. You told me you would. Then I didn't hear from you again. Now it's three days later and you're trying to hide from me. You mind telling me what's been going on in that piss-poor excuse of a brain of yours?"

Mark's mouth opened.

His jaw moved up and down.

No words came out.

His uncle's big piledriver of a fist smashed across his jaw, pain exploding in his head as he went flying backward. After he crashed to the floor, he wailed in agony and made no immediate attempt to get to his feet because it wouldn't have been possible. He heard the heavy, unhurried clomping of his uncle's work boots on the floor as he came closer.

Mark whimpered when he saw the man looming above him.

He raised a shaky hand in a pitiful warding-off gesture.

"D-don't . . . puh-please . . ."

James Castleberry scowled. "Fucking stupid-ass pussy."

He lifted his nephew off the floor and this time backhanded him across the face, causing Mark to stagger toward the bed and fall upon it. The backhand blow was, if anything, delivered with more force than the direct crash of knuckles against his jaw. At least one tooth was loose now. He felt blood filling the inside of his mouth and tried spitting it out. Something about this disgusted his uncle enough to make more derogatory comments. Mark couldn't help it, though. He felt like he was choking on blood. His tongue touched the loose tooth, igniting another spark of agony.

Tears filled Mark's eyes as his uncle loomed over him again. "You . . . you can't do this to me," he said, squeezing the words out between whimpers. "I'm not a little kid anymore. I'm all . . . I'm all grown up now."

James Castleberry snorted derisively. "Bullshit. You ain't no man. A man doesn't let some bitch punk his ass like that. You're still a boy in that weak head of yours. I'm almost glad your daddy ain't still around to see what a pansy-ass you've become. But I'm gonna do right by my brother's memory by whipping that weakness out of you. It's long overdue."

He began to reach for his nephew.

Mark squealed in fright and frantically scooted backward on the bed, not stopping until the top of his head butted up against the head-board. He was breathing hard as he sat up and said, "I killed a girl."

His uncle had one knee up on the mattress and was in the process of drawing his fist back again to deliver another devastating blow when Mark impulsively blurted out the confession. The fist remained suspended in the air above him for several seconds.

Then the older man slowly lowered his hand, unclenching the fist. The look on his face was a dubious one. "The fuck did you say?"

Mark swallowed a lump in his throat and struggled to get his breathing back into a regular rhythm. "It's true. I swear. I killed a girl before I left Virginia." A burst of nervous laughter stuttered out of him. "Stabbed the shit out of her. Would a weak person do that?"

James Castleberry spent some time studying his nephew's face, searching it for signs of falsehood. He grunted. "A weak person might do anything under the right circumstances. Once. On the spur of the moment. You think I haven't killed some cunts?" He sneered, laughing as he shook his head. "Shee-it. I used to do it all the time up and down the coast back in my trucker days. I've got at least a dozen dead lot lizards to my name. Plus maybe a dozen more random fuckers buried out on my property."

Now it was Mark's turn to carefully study the other man's expression. At first he thought maybe his uncle was just being boastful or trying to one-up him. He didn't doubt the man had killed some people in his time. Maybe even a hooker or two. He had more than enough rage in him.

But was he an actual serial killer?

The man's steady, unblinking gaze was pretty convincing.

James Castleberry smiled when he saw belief dawn in his nephew's eyes. "Okay, kid. So you killed a bitch. I'm guessing this was your first time?"

Mark swallowed hard again and nodded. "Yeah."

James grunted. "All right. So tell me all about it."

Mark's eyes flicked toward the table. "Could I maybe have one of those beers first?"

"Sure thing."

His uncle went over to the table and tore open the cardboard carton, bringing back two cans dripping with condensation. He handed one over to Mark and returned briefly to the table to grab a chair, plopping it down next to the bed.

James settled into the chair.

Mark started talking, telling the story of his first murder in vivid detail.

When he was done, his uncle stared at him in sullen silence for a long time, his expression slowly sharpening, exuding a dangerous level of anger. Different parts of his face started to twitch. That was never a good sign. Mark was close to whimpering again when the man abruptly leapt out of his chair. The sound of crumpling aluminum as the beer can flattened against his nose was not unfamiliar in this context. He'd been hit with them countless times in his younger days.

He screamed in terror as James Castleberry hauled him up off the bed and stood him up against the sink basin outside the bathroom. A barrage of heavy blows from the man's big fists battered his lower back. The first few punches were bad enough, but after that, they started feeling like they were going right through him. Horrible stabbing pains lanced his insides. He felt like he'd die if it went on much longer. Worst of all, he was as powerless to fight off the assault as he'd been when he was a kid. It was humiliating.

The beating finally stopped.

Mark sobbed as he dropped to his knees and held onto the edge of the basin.

His uncle's voice was thick with contempt as he said, "Killing that bitch was some stupid shit, boy. Even by your low standards. It'll be a goddamn miracle if the police don't wind up connecting you to it. You want to get away with murder, you don't go after bitches like that. Go after whores and bar sluts. The ones nobody gives a damn about. Jesus. What a goddamn idiot you are."

Mark's voice hitched in his throat. "I . . . I know."

A brief silence ensued.

Then James Castleberry sighed and dug a scrap of paper out of his hip pocket. He pushed the scrap into one of his nephew's hands, making sure it was clenched tight around it.

"That's the address for the bitch who stole your tape. I had no choice but to start looking for her myself when you went radio silent. Wasn't even that hard. She took her socials down and her friends went quiet online, but they all have acquaintances who apparently didn't get the fucking memo. I found plenty of tagged pictures. That gave me enough info to plug into some reverse lookup sites and get what we needed. Your girl's real name is Allison Cook. She lives in Ohio."

Still trembling badly, Mark unclenched his hand and looked at the scrap of paper. "So . . . we're going to Ohio?"

James snorted. "*We're* not doing shit. You're gonna be on your own. The Visitor was originally my burden. I got free of him by shifting that shit to you. I don't want it coming back on me, which is what's gonna happen if you don't get that tape back. This is your responsibility. I expect you to shape up and take care of it like a man."

Mark sniffled and turned his head to look at his uncle. "You told me we'd take care of her together. Cut her up in pieces and dump her in a landfill."

James shook his head. "That was before you told me about the stupid shit you did in Virginia. I ain't gonna be in your vicinity if shit takes another bad turn." He went to the door and opened it, standing there with his hand on the doorknob a moment longer. "I expect that bitch to be dead by the end of the week. You hear me? Don't bother coming home if you can't get it done."

He left then, slamming the door shut behind him.

Mark fell onto his side on the floor, shivering as he curled up into a ball.

He cried for a long time.

FIFTEEN

ALLISON WAS STILL BLEARY-EYED and more than a little fuzzy-headed when she got up and discovered the *Homecoming* tape was not still inside the VCR, where she expected to find it. Her brain needed more time to get even close to peak operating condition and thus it took a while for the full implications of this development to sink in, and even when that happened, she needed an even longer while to start believing it.

Cassie was gone when she woke up, which did not alarm her. Staying the night likely meant there were things she'd delayed doing, so of course she would want to get a jump on catching up. Leaving without waking her to say goodbye was also not a surprising thing. That was a case of showing basic consideration for a person obviously in dire need of a deep and prolonged rest.

Later, of course, she would realize Cassie had other reasons for not waking her prior to departing.

She'd put on a pot of coffee when she realized she had no memory of removing the videotape from the VCR. The trash can next to the kitchen counter was overflowing with empty bottles. A check of the fridge confirmed that all the beer purchased yesterday was gone. Also missing were various stray leftover beers from previous purchases, ones that went unconsumed for a long time because she wound up not caring much for them. She'd kept this mixture of cans and bottles in one of the door compartments. All gone now. Judging from the rotten way she felt, she probably drank most of them herself.

Maybe she didn't remember putting the tape away because she had blank spots in her memory from overconsumption. Perhaps she'd even half-dreamed about it being gone while still in that deeper semi-groggy state.

Maybe it was actually still there.

She wobbled out of the kitchen and to the living room, staggering her way over to the old Zenith and the VCR atop it. It took a few shaky stabs at the eject button to get the top-loader to pop up out of the VCR.

When it finally did, she found it still empty.

Well, fuck.

Allison frowned.

She turned slowly around and scanned the rest of the living room, starting with the glass-topped coffee table. Then she searched her bookcases.

No sign of the tape.

By then her head was starting to clear ever-so-slightly, which created an opening for the first faint flickers of panic to start creeping in. Moving somewhat more steadily by that point, she walked out of the living room and down a short hallway to her bedroom. The first thing she did there was check the dresser drawer where she'd previously stashed the tape beneath a pile of undies. Not there. Heart rate accelerating, she hurriedly rifled through all the other drawers of the dresser, including ones where she'd never consider stashing something as precious as that tape.

The tape wasn't in the dresser.

Panic intensified.

A quiet little whimper escaped her lips. "Oh, no. Oh, no."

She dropped to her knees and checked under the bed, pulling out a box where she kept some self-pleasure items. No tape in there or anywhere else under the bed. Shoving the box back into its normal place, she got to her feet and swept the pillows away from the bed. Finding an item of such importance there was unlikely, but at that point she was becoming desperate. She commenced a deep and frantic search of her overstuffed little closet, again turning up nothing.

Allison was close to literally tearing her hair out as she ran out of the bedroom and back to the kitchen. She had handfuls of hair clutched tightly in her hands as she tried hard to choke back the anguished scream that wanted to come. In the kitchen, she rooted through the trash, dumping empty beer bottles, soiled paper plates, and other things on the floor.

No tape in the trash.

This time she did scream.

In frustration, she punched the plastic trash can, knocking it over. More trash spilled out on the floor. She was making a disgusting mess, but she was too frantic with worry to care. Springing back to her feet, she made another circuit of the house, double-checking everywhere she'd already looked and searching every nook and cranny she missed the first time.

Again, nothing.

Tears spilled down her face as she again ran back to the bedroom. Her phone was on the little bedside table. She hadn't checked it for messages yet. Grabbing it, she hit the home button, lighting up the screen. There were a few trivial messages from online acquaintances she texted with on an irregular basis, but nothing from Cassie.

Maybe her friend had some idea where she'd put the tape before crashing for the night. It was probably in some crazy random spot she'd never think of putting it while sober. Maybe Cassie saw her do it and could fill in the memory gap for her. At that point, the darkest possibility still had not occurred to her. She sent Cassie a quick text with the basic details and awaited a response.

More than ten minutes later, she was still waiting.

Allison frowned as she sat on the edge of the bed.

What the fuck?

The long response time was not like her friend at all.

Cassie didn't have a job, at least not in the traditional sense. Because of her striking looks and natural strong sense for fashion, she was that rare person who actually managed to make a good living as an online influencer. Various companies gave her money and free shit for promoting their products on her social media feeds. Her time was largely her own, which meant she was almost always able to answer texts or return calls on a timely basis. This was often the case even when she was attending some promo event or posing for photographers.

Not hearing from her after ten minutes was unusual.

Still not hearing from her after twenty was actively worrisome.

At that point, Allison sent a second, longer text, in which she was far more emphatic about her state of distress.

Another ten minutes went by.

Nothing.

Allison screeched in frustration.

She stood up and stamped a foot on the floor.

Her first attempt to call Cassie went straight to voicemail, as did the next several attempts. Stranger and stranger. It occurred to her to wonder if something had happened to her friend. Maybe she was hurt or in the hospital. The prospect was terrifying. She had no other friends as close to her as Cassie. Even the remote possibility of losing her filled her with dread.

And then the dark thing finally occurred to her.

What if there was another reason for the lack of response?

What if Cassie took *Homecoming* with her when she left?

This was another possibility that made her sick to her core, one she could scarcely wrap her mind around at all. Her best friend in the whole world stealing something that important to her was inconceivable, an idea that would offend her deeply if suggested by anyone else.

And yet, what else made any sense?

She spent a few additional minutes stewing over it while intermittently checking her phone for a belated response.

No such response ever came.

By then she knew what she had to do.

SIXTEEN

STILL IN THE CLOTHES SHE'D worn the night before, Allison slipped on some shoes, grabbed her keys and purse, and headed down the hallway to the living room. A quick exit from the house was her sole focus in those frenzied moments

Before she could enter the living room and go to the front door, however, some instinct made her glance back down the hallway. That instinct was almost like a whisper in her ear, a tickle of cold breath that made her shiver. When she looked back, for a second she thought she glimpsed a slender figure standing at the far end of the hallway, right outside her open bedroom door. She gasped and dropped her keys. They landed with a clatter on the hardwood floor.

Her body went rigid with fright.

She blinked and the figure disappeared. Or maybe it'd never really been there at all. Maybe what she'd seen was only a product of a mind overdriven with stress and still suffering from insufficient rest. Some form of fleeting hallucination was the only sensible explanation, because there was no way the man with the melting face could possibly have stepped out of her dreams and into her waking life. In the dreams, the figure was connected to the tape in some indefinable way that was not explicitly spelled out. It was something she understood on an elemental level.

Maybe the melting man wanted the tape back.

Maybe he was angry with her for losing track of it.

Or maybe she was losing her goddamn mind a little bit here.

Angry with herself now, she pushed past her fear and stalked back down the hallway. She was being ridiculous. Ghostly figures from realms beyond didn't exist in real life. And if they did, they didn't materialize in the daytime. Not normally, anyway. Anyone who watched horror movies knew that. Yes, she'd hypothesized about some wild things last night, but she was completely sober now and back in the land of reality.

She looked into her bedroom.

No creepy melting man figure in there, either.

She heaved a big breath, allowed herself another moment to calm her nerves, and quickly headed back down the hallway. Another tickle of phantom cold breath made her shiver again, but this time she didn't glance backward. She snatched up her keys, hurried through the living room, and went out the front door.

Her blue Chevy Cruze was parked in the short driveway.

She dropped in behind the wheel, dumped her purse on the passenger seat, and jabbed at the ignition button. The engine came to life with a smooth automotive purr. She put the car in reverse and stomped on the gas pedal. An instant later, she had to hit the brake when she heard the honking of a horn in the street. As the Cruze squealed to a stop, she glanced at the rearview mirror in time to see a big heavy-duty pickup truck go flashing by. She also saw someone wagging an upraised middle finger at her through the truck's open passenger side window.

She put a hand to her chest and felt the hammering of her heart.

Jesus fucking Christ.

She'd come within a whisker of getting herself pancaked. A brief moment of awful clarity intruded as understanding of how close she'd come to getting crippled or killed fully penetrated. She imagined her parents—from whom she was more or less estranged at this point— having to plan her funeral. Would they even have one for her? If so, how many would attend? She guessed maybe five or six people might be there, her parents included.

All because she was so desperate to reclaim a videotape she herself had stolen from another person. It was insane, undeniably, and on an intellectual level she understood that entirely.

She wanted it back anyway.

Her second attempt to back out of the driveway was calmer and more successful. Cassie lived in an apartment building in the same suburb of Columbus Allison had called home the last four years. She knew the way there by heart, so well she believed she could make the drive there blindfolded if necessary. Her brush with death compelled a more moderate speed than what she'd originally planned. Even so, the drive over there didn't take long.

She spotted her friend's red Versa even before pulling into the parking lot. The car was parked facing the breezeway that stood between halves of the four-unit building. There was some level of relief in seeing the car there. It meant she wouldn't have to go hunting around town, looking for Cassie in her many regular haunts. But trepidation remained, her anxiety surging at the prospect of confronting her over the apparent theft. The accusation was one she didn't want to make, but what choice did she have?

Maybe there was an explanation.

Some good reason Cassie might have taken the tape.

One that wouldn't make her heart ache.

She sure fucking hoped so anyway.

Allison left her purse on the passenger seat as she got out of her car. She was already racing for the breezeway as the door slammed shut. Cassie lived in one of the upstairs units. These apartments were spacious inside, with nearly as much interior square footage as her little house. The rent wasn't cheap, even though the building was old. Cassie didn't mind because she had money to burn. She often said she'd only move out when she finally felt ready to make her long-planned move to L.A.

A thumping race up the metal stairs and then she was standing outside the door to Cassie's place. She was breathing hard and her heart was in dangerous overdrive. Her stomach was twisting, tortured by a combination of skyrocketing anxiety and lingering consequences from her night of overindulgence. She felt like she might faint or vomit or both if she couldn't get herself under control soon.

She pounded on the door with the base of a fist.

"Cassie!"

A minute passed.

The door didn't open.

Allison pounded on the door again, harder this time. Another silent moment elapsed, then she heard a muffled curse from the other side of the door. Though the sound was faint, she recognized the timbre of that voice.

Cassie was here and she was awake.

Another moment passed and then she heard a sound of footsteps. Next came the sound of the door unlocking. It creaked as it came a couple inches away from the frame. Her friend's face appeared in the gap, with the gold-plated lock chain still in place.

Cassie's face was as flat and impassive as Allison had ever seen it. "What do you want?"

That annoyed tone.

Allison had never heard anything quite like it from her friend. Not directed at her, at least.

"You know what I want. Give it back."

Cassie grunted. "No."

She started to close the door.

Allison jammed a foot into the gap, stopping her before the door could fully close.

A sliver of Cassie's face appeared in the narrow gap again. "Take your fucking foot out of my door, Allison."

Tears welled in Allison's eyes. "Why are you doing this? *How* could you do it? You're my best friend."

A hint of a cruel smile appeared at the visible corner of Cassie's mouth. "That's right, I'm your best friend. The thing is, you're not *my* best friend. You're just one of so many. Honestly, you feel like only an acquaintance sometimes. I only hang out with you out of pity. You must know that." She laughed, seeing the deep hurt on Allison's face. "I took the tape because I could. The tape wanted me to take it."

Allison frowned as her tears flowed hotter and faster. "What?"

Cassie sighed. "I'm tired of talking to you. The tape is mine now. Accept it. Now take your foot out of my door before I call the police."

Allison angrily swiped away tears. "Go ahead. I'll tell them you stole from me."

Cassie's laugh was louder now, with a nastier edge. "Yeah, you do that, bitch. Tell them about how I stole some moldy old videotape you stole from somebody else. They won't give a shit. And they'll laugh at you as they drag you away."

A moment of tense silence went by.

Then Cassie said, "Your other option is that I open this door, come out there, and throw your scrawny ass down the stairs. Go ahead. Test me. See if I won't do it."

The look on what she could see of Cassie's face convinced Allison she meant what she was saying.

On the verge of sobbing, she took her foot out of the gap.

The door slammed in her face.

SEVENTEEN

MARK GOT OUT ON THE road early Wednesday morning. He wasn't able to leave Tuesday night because he was in too much agony from the beating delivered by his uncle. There was blood in his urine and his insides felt like they were repeatedly being jabbed by dozens of hot needles. The pain was so bad he went to the motel's desk clerk and begged him for tips on where he might score some OxyContins in the area. Turned out he was already in the right place. The clerk sold him ten generic pills at ten dollars a pop, which was a bargain. He figured the guy took one look at his sweaty face and took pity on him.

He stumbled back to his room and washed three pills down with a can of Budweiser, hoping that would be enough to get him to sleep. Ideally, he'd be heading out to the highway already. Given the narrow time frame decreed by his uncle, losing an entire night of travel time would put him behind in a big way, but an extended period of high-way driving simply wasn't within the realm of possibility at that point. Not even close, really. A recovery period was an absolute necessity. He'd have to make up the lost time as best he could once he was finally on the road.

The pills made him woozy. He faded in and out of consciousness numerous times, but slipping into a prolonged period of uninterrupted sleep proved an elusive goal. Eventually, he got frustrated enough to get up and take one more pill with another can of Bud. He was trying to be careful and maintain at least some slight pretense of rationing the pills. An accidental overdose was the last thing he wanted at this point, which in a way was funny, given how much time he'd spent immersed in suicidal ideation after leaving Virginia.

Things had changed.

He no longer wanted to kill himself. Not yet, anyway. Not until he'd taken care of that thieving chick. Not until the tape was back in his possession. Also, while these things were important to him, there was another motivating factor, maybe the biggest of them all. He didn't want to die until after he'd gotten revenge against his uncle. After enduring so many years of physical and psychological abuse at that man's hands, some form of payback was long overdue.

He'd have to kill the fucker.

Anything short of that would be a massive mistake. He couldn't leave James Castleberry alive to seek retribution. If he did, the man would make him suffer for a long time before killing him, and Mark wanted no part of that. He knew what the bastard was capable of and had already suffered enough.

The fourth pill did the trick.

He slept without waking for around four and a half hours.

When he woke up, the pain was still there, but it was slightly more muted than before. He heaved himself off the bed and staggered over to the bathroom, where he was relieved to see less blood in his stream when he took a piss. After stripping off the clothes he'd slept in, he took a hot shower, got dressed again, and went back to the gas station across the street. This time he stocked up on energy drinks. Before leaving, he scored a small amount of coke from the desk clerk, just enough to give him a decent jump-start.

Out on the road, he drove fast in his black Mustang, but not too fast, keeping his speed within the range above the speed limit law enforcement considered generally acceptable. Of course, that range could vary some from jurisdiction to jurisdiction, but usually not in a drastic way. He listened to ominous synthwave music devoid of vocals to help keep his mind centered while he drove. The trip from his home in Carbondale to Hilliard was calculated at just over seven hours on his GPS app. He hoped to make it there in slightly less than that by keeping gas station pit stops to a bare minimum.

For the most part, he was able to adhere to this plan, but at one stop he had to wait outside the occupied men's room for almost twenty minutes. This period was sheer misery. He felt close to pissing his pants from the energy drinks. There was a line outside the women's room, so that wasn't an option. He was nearly to the point of leaving to urinate on the dumpster out back when the men's room door finally opened, and an elderly man in green golf pants and a pink button-up shirt shuffled out into the hallway.

Mark sneered as he pushed by the sheepish-looking old fart. "Hope you enjoyed your epic fucking shit, grandpa."

He locked the door and rushed over to the toilet, hurriedly unzipping his fly and taking out his dick in time to begin what he subsequently decided was easily the longest-lasting single incidence of urination in his entire damn life. By the time the last few drops dribbled into the bowl, he felt like Mike Myers in the first *Austin Powers* movie, that scene where the title character wakes up after decades of being cryogenically frozen and subsequently takes the longest piss in movie history. Only this real-life equivalent to that wasn't nearly as amusing. He felt pain in his bladder as it emptied, another lingering consequence of the previous night's pummeling. Right then and there, he made a vow to piss on his uncle's corpse before dissolving it in a pit of lye.

After zipping up, he headed to the sink to wash his hands, but before he could stick them under the faucet, he felt a strange chill at the back of his neck. Knowing he would see The Visitor standing behind him if he looked at the mirror above the sink, he forced his eyes to stay away from it.

To his surprise, the interdimensional being had left him alone in the days since the theft of the *Homecoming* tape. He'd expected a sharp increase in the frequency and intensity of materializations, but there'd been no contact at all. There was only that background presence that was always in his head, but after years of that being there, he was mostly able to ignore it. Sometimes he could pretend like it wasn't there at all. The physical visitations were different—and far more frightening. When they happened, a helpless physical reaction of deep repulsion would occur. There'd be a sensation of fat worms crawling under his skin and slithering around in his stomach. The chill he felt intensified until he felt like he was standing naked on a patch of arctic ice.

Keeping his gaze directed at the porcelain basin, Mark cleared his throat and spoke softly. "I'm sorry I lost your gift, but I swear I'll get it back. I know where the bitch who took it is. I'm on my way there now. I promise you, this will never happen again."

The air in the bathroom grew sharply colder.

He felt a soft exhalation of freezing breath on the nape of his neck. The feather-light touch of a phantom finger tickled him there.

Mark yelped in fright and ran out of the bathroom.

He didn't stop running until he was back outside. As he stood next to his Mustang, that sense of being observed by something alien to this world was gone, as was the chill at the back of his neck. His hand trembled as he opened the driver side door and slipped in behind the wheel.

After a brief hesitation, he glanced at the rearview mirror, letting out a relieved breath when he failed to see The Visitor in the backseat.

He started the car and raced back out to the highway.

EIGHTEEN

IN THE WAKE OF CASSIE'S stunning and unexpected act of betrayal, Allison was too distraught to function in any normal manner. Wednesday was the day of her scheduled return to work at the call center, but that did not come to pass. She called in sick, leaving a tearful and not entirely intelligible voicemail for her supervisor. The one thing she was clear about in the message was that something traumatic had happened and she did not expect to return to work until the following Monday.

She would get in trouble for that, maybe even get written up, but Allison's mental state at that point was so fragile she didn't give much of a damn. Her record after years of working at that place was exemplary. Never written up, never late. Not even once. They wouldn't be happy about this, but they wouldn't fire her over it either. Might be another matter if she failed to show up next week as well, but she'd worry about that when the time came.

After having the door slammed shut in her face at Cassie's place, she reluctantly returned to her house, where she spent hours crying and moping over the situation. While the apparent loss of the one friendship in her life she'd viewed as deep and meaningful hurt, she was even more upset over the loss of the videotape. Other people might view that as an indictment of her shortcomings as a human being, but she saw no point in denying the truth to herself.

She was a horror fan in general and loved tons of other films in the genre, but the *Friday* franchise held a special place in her heart. When she was a sullen teenager with no friends and parents who didn't understand her, those movies provided a strange kind of comfort she found in little else. Her dad straight-up told her he thought there was something wrong with her for liking those movies, a wound that cut deep and never healed. That only made her cling to the films even more fiercely. She saw a little something of herself in Jason, venting his anguish against the cool kids who scorned him during his mortal life. It was therapy and catharsis. She had no desire to hurt other people, but through watching Jason go through his murderous paces she could vicariously purge herself of those bad feelings.

These were things she came to understand better when she was older and more self-reflective, but even back then it was something she knew on an intuitive level. She would feel bad about things in general and then she'd watch, say, *The Final Chapter* and feel much better. Not too hard a connection to make. They meant the world to her, those movies, but even for a serious devotee such as herself, the threat of burnout always loomed these days. She'd seen all the movies in the series countless times, at well over a hundred viewings for her favorite installments. Even the ones she didn't love quite as much as the others were beyond over-familiar at this point.

For a host of complicated reasons, most having to do with years of legal wrangling between various parties, there'd been no new movies in the series since 2009. She wasn't yet thirty—though that milestone was coming up soon—so that was a big chunk of her life spent waiting for another one. She often wondered if there'd *ever* be a new *Friday* movie. That was a depressing thought. That 2009 reboot was the only one she'd ever seen while it was new in a theater. Having that experience again, at least one more time, had for years been her fondest wish.

She'd begun to lose hope of that ever happening until, out of nowhere, a stranger showed her a vintage *Friday the 13th* movie she'd never known existed. An impossible thing somehow manifested into reality by means she'd likely never understand. That fact alone made the film a precious, one-of-a-kind artifact, but even more amazingly it was a genuinely great *Friday* sequel, one of the absolute best in the series.

Cassie knew her as well as anyone ever had.

And she damn well knew how much *Homecoming* meant to her. So this was no ordinary betrayal. It went way beyond just taking something from her. This was more akin to ripping out her heart and showing it to her while it was still beating. And then laughing about it.

No matter how much she thought about it, Allison still couldn't begin to understand how Cassie could have done this to her.

She made more calls that went straight to voicemail.

Sent more texts that went unanswered.

You didn't have to do this. I could've made you a copy.

Please, please, please let me make a copy.

You want money? I can give you money. Thousands. Every penny of my savings. I just want the fucking movie back.

And so on.

Each new message more desperate than the last.

At last, after so many hours lost in abject, tearful misery, anger became the more dominant emotion. She relinquished her grip on the Jason Voorhees pillow and crawled out of bed to stumble off to the bathroom. The sight of her bleary, tear-streaked face in the mirror above the sink further stoked her anger. Someone she'd thought loved and respected her had done this incalculably callous and hurtful thing to her. Even worse, that person probably felt secure in believing there was nothing Allison could do about it.

She sneered at her reflection.

We'll just have to see about that.

She swallowed some Tylenol to vanquish the lingering hangover headache still plaguing her and took a shower. After the shower, she donned plain black clothes—leggings and a t-shirt—with no logos or images on them. She put her hair in a ponytail and wedged a black ball cap into place on her head. The goal was to look anonymous, but when she checked herself out in the long mirror in her bedroom, she realized she looked like a burglar.

Too conspicuous.

She removed the hat.

Besides, she wasn't even sure yet what she had in mind. She doubted anything of consequence would happen today. Somewhere in her head was a vague notion of reclaiming the tape by any means necessary, but any direct effort to do so would probably have to wait for another day, when she was better prepared. Right now she needed to get out of the house and feel like she was at least taking action in some small way.

She got in her car and drove back to Cassie's apartment.

Traffic was thicker this time of day. Getting over to Cassie's place took closer to fifteen minutes. This time she only drove by the building instead of pulling into the little parking lot out front. There was no sign of Cassie's red Versa. The only car in the lot was a green Prius she knew belonged to another resident, a middle-aged woman with whom her now former friend did not get along.

Allison drove another block and turned down a side street. From there she was able to cross back over and pull into an alley that ran behind Cassie's building. The alley was bordered by a tall wooden privacy fence on one side and a shorter chain-link fence on the other. The privacy fence hid the backyard of a house while the chain-link fence acted as a barrier against entry into the area behind the apartment building. In theory. Scaling it wouldn't be a problem, if it came to that. Several windows overlooked this area, but the blinds in most of them were closed. As far as she could tell, no one was peeking out back at this particular moment, which was unsurprising. The view in this direction wasn't an especially pleasing or stimulating one. There was a dumpster in this area, as well as a rarely used picnic table and a tool shed. Right now, as usual, the area was devoid of people.

She wished like hell Cassie lived in one of the ground floor units. If she did, it'd be tempting to take action this very moment. Drive down to the end of the alley and park at the curb on the side street, then jog back, vault herself over the fence, and smash out one of those back windows. Climb inside and hunt around until she located the tape. Knowing the interior of the place as well as she did, it probably wouldn't take very long.

Unfortunately, that was not the reality she was facing.

She looked up at the back windows of Cassie's second floor unit and sighed in frustration. Getting up there would require an extendable ladder, which was something she didn't have. She supposed she could go buy one, but she had no serious intention of doing that. Even envisioning the process of buying a big ladder, transporting it over here in her little car, and then everything else she'd have to do after heaving the ladder over the fence was a laughably absurd exercise in futility.

There had to be a better way to get into Cassie's place.

A *simpler* way.

She was thinking about the old-fashioned crowbar in the garage back at her house when a horn honked directly behind her. The sound made her gasp and flinch. A check of the rearview mirror showed her a long-haired young-ish guy behind the wheel of an older model Hyundai. He made a hurry-up-and-move waving motion with his hands when he saw her looking at the mirror. Allison felt foolish. She'd been so lost in thought she hadn't heard the other vehicle pull up behind her. It was almost funny, in a way. A person hoping to commit a successful act of burglary would need much better situational awareness than what she'd shown here.

She drove out of the alley and circled back around for another view of the front of the building.

Cassie's red Versa was back.

In fact, she was getting out of it right as Allison drove by.

And someone else was getting out on the passenger side. She wasn't able to glimpse the other person, because as soon as she saw Cassie, she hit the gas and sped away. Her heart was thumping and her hands were locked tight around the wheel. She didn't start to slow down until she neared a red light three more blocks up the street, at which point she stomped on the brake and brought the Cruze to a squealing stop.

Regret assailed her, causing her to scream through her teeth. Instead of speeding away like a coward, she should have whipped into that parking lot and jumped out to confront Cassie. Even now a part of her was urging her to turn around and race back there, but she didn't do it because the moment of fleeting opportunity was already gone.

She was almost back to her house when her phone rang.

She took it out of the cupholder between the front seats and glanced at the screen, tensing up when she saw Cassie's name. The phone rang twice more while she held her breath and stared at that name, hesitating.

Then she hit the accept call button and put the phone to her ear. "Hello?"

She winced at the meekness in her tone, at the groveling weakness right below the surface.

Cassie barked harsh laughter. "I saw you creeping by my place, bitch. Thought you were being such a stealthy little cunt, didn't you?" More of that harsh laughter. "What's funny is I was thinking of taking pity on you. I thought maybe I'd have one of my nerdy guy friends make a copy of that tape for you. No lie. I really was. But that's not gonna happen now. You show your face around here again, you'll regret it. You might even wind up in the hospital. Stay the fuck away, you creepy bitch. Or else."

The line went dead.

Allison was sobbing uncontrollably by the time she pulled into her driveway.

NINETEEN

CASSIE STARED AT HER PHONE for several moments after angrily stabbing at the red end call button with her index finger. The phone was gripped tightly in her shaking hand. She was so upset she could almost imagine crushing it like some dimwitted frat boy crumpling an empty beer can. The things she'd said to Allison played back in her head like a recording of some unhinged stranger. It was hard to believe they'd emerged from her own mouth and yet there was no denying they had. For a moment she was gripped by an intense urge to ring Allison back and say how sorry she was, but she didn't do it, because she knew she'd just wind up frothing at the mouth again.

What the fuck is wrong with me?

Before she could ponder the question further, she heard the sound of a toilet flushing followed by the opening of a creaky door. Not a lot of time passed between the two sounds, which led her to believe her guest hadn't washed his hands.

Gross.

Floorboards in the hallway creaked and seconds later Darren Bateman came back into the living room. He'd announced an urgent need to urinate not long after they'd entered Cassie's apartment together. Not surprising given how quickly he'd guzzled down a gas station fountain soda approximately as big as his head, which was quite big indeed.

Darren was a big guy in general, tall-ish at just a shade under six feet and with the pudgy physique that came with spending the large majority of one's life seated firmly in front of one kind of screen or other. The legs of his loose-fitting blue shorts were so long they were almost more like pants and his ancient *Watchmen* t-shirt looked like it was one washing away from dissolving and becoming a pile of dust.

He looked askance at Cassie as he began to move past her. "Pardon my eavesdropping, but did I hear a reference to your 'nerdy guy friends'? Because I may or may not somewhat resemble that remark."

Her iron grip on the phone relaxed as she turned and watched Darren approach her entertainment center. "You heard that?"

Down on one knee now, he glanced at her as he began uncoiling some of the cables he'd brought with him. Also on the floor with him was an old VCR he'd referred to as a portable model, though it was so bulky this seemed a ludicrous term for it. He adjusted his large-frame glasses and shrugged. "You sort of screamed it."

Cassie grunted. "I need you to do something for me."

He squinted behind the glasses. "You mean something other than copying that movie for you?"

"Here's the thing about that," she said, her tone sharper and nastier than she intended, but she wasn't in a great mood, so the hell with it. "I no longer want that, so I'm gonna need you to get out of my fucking apartment."

He stared at her with his mouth hanging open a moment, while still slowly unraveling a cable. "What, seriously?"

She nodded, a grim look on her face. "Yes, I'm afraid so."

He looked at the wires and things he'd brought with him before sighing and saying, "Okay."

"I'm sorry, I know it's an inconvenience, but it's been a weird, fucked-up kind of day, and I'm in a massively pissy mood. I need to be alone for a while, starting right the fuck now."

Darren shrugged. "Understood. If you change your mind, let me know."

After stowing the cables away in a backpack, he stood up, hoisting the portable VCR by its attached strap. He pulled the strap up over his shoulder and accompanied Cassie to the front door. She opened the door and he stepped outside, turning toward her on the breezeway landing.

She started to close the door. "Sorry again. Thank you for

understanding."

His eyes widened behind the glasses. "Whoa, wait!" His hand shot out, stopping the door before it could fully close. "Aren't you driving me back?"

Her expression hardened. "What am I, your fucking chaperone? Get an Uber like a normal person and take your hand off my goddamn door."

He frowned as he took his hand away. "Wow. You *are* in a pissy mood."

"Told you."

She closed the door and locked it, feeling mildly proud of herself for not slamming it shut. At least she was still capable of exercising a little restraint, despite the abundance of proof to the contrary she'd exhibited throughout the day. That she'd taken the tape from Allison's place still seemed so unreal to her, like something she couldn't possibly have actually done, yet she'd done it just the same. The worst thing about it wasn't the act of thievery itself. She was an honest person at heart and had never been prone to doing such things, so she'd feel bad about stealing from anyone. No, the worst thing about this nefarious deed by far was the matter of from whom she'd stolen.

Allison was like a sister to her. Hell, she was closer to her than her own flesh and blood sister, a blonde corporate ice queen who looked down on her and liked to make snooty, cutting remarks about her "lack of direction" at all the infrequent family gatherings.

All the things she'd said to Allison today to make her feel small and unimportant were terrible lies. The words felt like poison in her mouth, but she said them anyway.

All because of that fucking tape.

The theft was an unplanned, spontaneous event.

Allison was still out like a rock when Cassie woke up next to her in bed. She was clutching her Jason pillow and snoring away, sounding very much like someone who wouldn't be up for hours yet. Slipping quietly out of bed, Cassie donned a pair of her friend's pajama pants and one of her black horror shirts. The dress she'd worn the night before was on a hanger in Allison's closet. At that point, she had no intention of leaving any time soon. Her schedule was clear for the day and her time was her own. No reason for haste. When she walked out of the bedroom, it was with the thought of heading to the kitchen to scramble some eggs.

Instead, a seemingly random impulse sent her out to the living room, where she went straight to the vintage television and punched the VCR's eject button. The top-loader popped up with the *Homecoming* tape still inside it. She didn't realize she'd been holding her breath until she removed the tape and held it in her hands. An electric tingle went up her arms as soon as her fingers touched the plastic. She felt transfixed by the object in her hands, a thing that looked so ordinary at first glance, just an obsolete relic from a long-ago time, but that surface ordinariness was an illusion. What it actually felt like was an enchanted object from a fairy tale, a thing as precious and rare as buried treasure. She didn't know if it was actually from another world or reality, as Allison had theorized, but when she held it in her hands, any magical or otherwise fanciful explanation felt possible.

She stood there and stared at it for what felt like a long time but was probably only a few minutes, the desire to possess it—to have it only to herself—taking shape within her well before she was even aware it was happening. Looking back now, of course, it struck her as deeply strange she should become so single-mindedly obsessed with it so quickly. The logical option of asking Allison to dub a copy of it for her—something her friend would happily have done—never once crossed her mind.

An urgent desire to take the tape and get out of the house before Allison could wake seized her, spurring her into hurried action. In those moments, she gave no thought to the inevitable ramifications of what she was doing. It was a little like being possessed by a ghost or demon. She ran into the kitchen and shoved the tape into her purse, snapping it shut. Next she hurried back to the bedroom, where she paused in the doorway to observe Allison, who was still obliviously snoring away. Cassie then quickly shed her borrowed clothes, retrieved her dress from the closet, and rushed out of the bedroom. A few minutes later, she was out of the house and speeding away in her car, her jittery nerves making her feel a bit like a bandit in the aftermath of some crazy heist.

Since then, she'd experienced considerable guilt and regret, some of it even before Allison's first anguished visit to her apartment. Almost right up to the moment the knock on her door came, she'd been trying to think of ways she might put things right. A mea culpa apology as she turned the tape over. An offer to make a copy of the tape. These potential gestures toward fairness all fled her head, however, the instant she opened the door and saw Allison standing there. The strange obsession reasserted itself, and along with it came a bitter sense of defensiveness. A willingness to justify anything at all in service of keeping the tape to herself. Once again, it was like being possessed.

Not long after ushering Darren out the door, Cassie went into her bedroom, opened the door to her closet, and took a shoebox down from the shelf. She carried the shoebox over to the bed, where she set it on the mattress and removed the lid with the reverence and awe of a devoutly religious person about to view some holy artifact.

There it was, nestled in layers of tissue paper.

A desire to immediately lift the tape out of the box was strong, almost impossible to resist, but she didn't give in to the impulse right away. Instead she stared at it and thought about all the horrible things she'd said to Allison today. Things she fervently wished she could take back. The tape's bizarre hold over her frightened her. It was a dangerous thing, regardless of how ordinary it looked. The smart thing would be to put the lid back on and carry the shoebox out back to the dumpster. Just drop it in and get fucking rid of it. Allison would be angry when she told her, but in time she'd see it was the right thing to do.

Cassie did not put the lid back on the shoebox.

With tears in her eyes, she reached into it and removed the tape from its nest of tissue paper, making a sound of almost sexual arousal when her fingers touched the plastic casing. She clutched the tape to her chest and wept a while. As the tearful episode began to ebb, she got numbly to her feet and carried it out to the living room.

Though she wasn't quite as obsessive or knowledgeable about it as people like Allison or Darren, Cassie also collected retro VHS. She had a few dozen tapes and a vintage VCR Allison had picked out at a thrift store and hooked up for her. It was a front-loading JVC from the late 80s.

Cassie put the tape in the machine, sat on her sofa, and used a remote to start the tape. She sat there and barely moved as she watched the movie that shouldn't exist all the way to the end.

When it was over, she hit the rewind button.

She stared at the empty black screen for a moment.

Then, sighing, she pushed play and the movie began again.

TWENTY

THERE WERE NO MORE ENCOUNTERS with The Visitor following the incident in the gas station bathroom. Mark was on edge for the entire last long stretch toward the Columbus area, afraid to even glance at the rearview for fear of seeing the spectral figure in the backseat of the Mustang. There were times when a glance at the mirror was unavoidable, such as when lane shifts were necessary at various junctures along the way. The relief he felt each time he saw it still wasn't there was a lifting of a massive mental burden, yet he was never able to savor the feeling for long, because the tension of dreadful expectation always began to mount again immediately.

Arriving in Hilliard without experiencing any additional otherworldly harassment felt like at least a minor miracle. Though he treasured the gifts he'd received as a result of his relationship with the enigmatic creature, he often found himself wishing for an end to it all, or even for it to never have started in the first place, but there was little he could do about it at this point.

As far as he knew, based on what he'd been told by his uncle, the only way to sever a psychic connection with The Visitor was by causing the creature to become interested in someone else, but a transference of the fixation wasn't easy. Sometimes it wasn't possible at all, regardless of how hard one tried. Again, this was according to his uncle, who many years earlier had unwittingly become the target of an attempted—and ultimately successful—transference. James Castleberry was then stuck with the thing until eventually causing it to become more interested in his nephew. Mark was especially vulnerable at the time, falling victim to his uncle's cruel psychological manipulation. After years of vicious abuse, the man made him think he was turning over a new leaf, starting with the sharing of an amazing secret.

Mark got so angry now when he thought about how easily he'd been duped. His life could've been so different in so many ways if not for his parents being murdered during a home invasion gone wrong. He was twelve at the time and only survived by hiding in the washing machine. The muffled sound of the gunshots that killed his mom and dad was something that still came back to him in random moments. The killers were never caught. His uncle took him in because there was no else willing to take on the burden. Any chance of a bright future ended right then and there. He was always going to wind up fucked in the head growing up in that man's house.

These were the things he thought about as he drove through the streets of Hilliard, following the directions of the voice navigator on his phone. A lot of depressing self-reflection. He wished he could go back in time and tell his younger self not to believe a word of his uncle's bullshit. He hadn't been a dumb kid, but at that point he'd been desperate for some sign of love and acceptance. And the worst part was how long it took him to realize the extent of his uncle's trickery. Years passed before he understood how dangerous The Visitor truly was. Even after he began to grasp the thing's essential malevolence, he persisted in believing the danger was easily manageable. This illusion was finally obliterated by his disastrous encounter with Allison Cook.

The Visitor would punish him if he couldn't retrieve the lost gift. Maybe even kill him.

Getting that tape back was his only hope.

Unless . . .

He frowned as he turned down the street where Allison lived. The GPS showed her house as two blocks straight ahead. A sense of nervous anticipation was already at work inside him, but now the feeling was tinged with an unexpected infusion of fresh possibility.

What if he could transfer The Visitor's fixation over to Allison?

Was that even possible?

He laughed.

Of course it was possible. The only question was whether he was capable of the same level of trickery and manipulation his uncle had used with him years ago. He wasn't sure about that. There were some obvious big differences between Allison and the kid he'd been back then. She was a grown woman who could probably smell bullshit from miles away. In his short time with her, he'd observed ample evidence of a mental toughness he hadn't possessed as a teenager. These things didn't mean an act of transference was impossible, but they would make it much harder.

His mind roiled with conflicting feelings on the subject. The prospect of living a life free of the creature's parasitic influence was a tempting one. He hadn't known what it was like to have a truly free life in a long time. It would be such a glorious, liberating thing.

On the other hand . . . no more gifts.

No more special movies.

He wasn't sure if liked that idea much at all. His collection of movies no one else in this world had ever seen was about the only thing that gave him any joy at all. Would life even feel worth living without it?

He didn't know, but the matter definitely warranted more consideration. There wasn't much time for that, though. He'd made his way to the home of the thief. Before the night was over, he would have to decide whether to kill her or attempt to ruin her life another way.

It was later in the afternoon as he drove slowly past Allison's small house. There was no car in the short driveway and the curtains in the front windows were drawn, with no sign of a light on inside. While he couldn't know for certain no one was home, his gut told him the place was empty.

He took a look around at the surrounding homes and saw no one out and about. No pedestrians walking down the street, no one sitting on a porch or doing yard work. He brought his car to a slow stop, letting it idle in the street as he pondered his next move. Initially he'd figured he'd do a quick drive-by, get a look at the place before heading elsewhere to kill some time until nightfall. Now, though, he was wondering if he should take advantage of the lack of activity in the area and do a little recon work.

Taking his foot off the brake, he goosed the Mustang's gas pedal until he reached the end of the block, where he pulled to the curb and parked in front of another house that appeared unoccupied. This one had a FOR SALE sign out front and no curtains in the windows. He felt he could safely leave his car here without arousing suspicion.

He got out and walked down the sidewalk back in the direction of Allison's house. His pace was unhurried. He kept his head up and his gaze straight ahead, trying his best to look like a local out for a walk. Someone with an easy way about him because he belonged here.

He stopped and took another look around as he reached Allison's house.

Still no one watching, at least that he could tell.

Around the side of the house, he was able to glimpse a slatted wooden fence. It was shorter than the tall privacy fences he saw around some of the other yards. Hopping over it would be no problem, should it come to that. He had no intention of trying anything like that while it was still daylight, of course. Just because he detected no obvious indications of being watched didn't mean he was safe. Some nosy busybody might peek out a window at the wrong moment, put in a call to the cops while he was unaware, and just like that everything would be ruined.

He could come back after dark and maybe break in through a back door or window. Smash his way in and try his damnedest to get to Allison before she could call 911 or run out the front door.

Mark was about to turn around and make his way back down the sidewalk to his car when he happened to glance at Allison's front door. He frowned, not sure if what he thought he was seeing was real or some subtle trick of light and shadow.

The door appeared slightly out of flush with the frame.

An impulse he was helpless to deny sent him up Allison's driveway and down a short sidewalk to her front porch. Even as he climbed the steps to the porch he could tell he'd been right. The door was not fully closed. Either someone was still inside or had left in a careless hurry, neglecting to fully close and lock the door. His impression of Allison was she wasn't the type to do the latter, but the lack of a car in the driveway made him wonder. He had no idea about her current state of mind. It was possible she was agitated or upset about something. Even an otherwise careful person might make this kind of oversight depending on the degree of upset involved.

He approached the door and stood there for several moments without taking action of any kind. His heart felt like it was beating too fast. He was scared. The fear struck him as absurd. Just two days ago he'd killed a person, yet here he was trembling and hesitating. It appeared that committing one terrible act didn't necessarily negate the natural reluctance of treading where one didn't belong. There was another difference, too. He didn't have a weapon on him this time. What if he went in there and found Allison at home after all? What if she had a gun?

Don't be a pussy. Open the goddamn door.

The thought was his own, but the voice in his head sounded an awful lot like James Castleberry.

Mark cringed as he heard the sound of an engine approaching. The car coming down the street likely was driven by some random passing motorist, but he couldn't know that for sure. Allison driving up and seeing him on her porch would be at least as disastrous as some nosy neighbor reporting him to the cops as a prowler.

There was no time to weigh the pros and cons of the matter.

He opened the door, stepped inside, and slammed it shut.

TWENTY-ONE

AFTER MORE THAN TWENTY MINUTES of sitting behind the wheel of her Cruze, the severe fit of sobbing at last began to ebb by slight degrees, the emotional agony relenting just a bit more every few minutes. By then late afternoon was beginning to edge toward early evening. Allison looked at the dashboard clock and felt a detached form of muted amazement, hardly able to believe a full half-hour had passed since she'd pulled into her driveway.

She wiped tears from her face and leaned back in her seat, not quite ready to get out of the car yet despite the slight abating of the storm still raging inside her. Her phone chimed. She took it out of the cupholder and saw a text from Julia, who wanted to know if Allison had heard from Cassie. She had something she wanted to ask her and couldn't get hold of her.

Allison sneered, shaking her head.

The vagueness meant they had plans that didn't include her. The fucked up thing about that was Allison couldn't even attribute that to today's drama. This sort of thing wasn't uncommon. She frequently didn't get invited to things where she would be an awkward presence, which encompassed about everything outside of horror cons and the times when the three of them would just hang out and watch movies. For the most part, she hadn't thought of the non-invitations as snubs.

In truth, she *was* awkward around regular people. On the rare occasions when she did go out drinking with them, some guy would inevitably try talking to her. They'd ask her what she liked to do for fun and tended to be weirded out when she'd only say, "Watch *Friday the 13th* movies. Collect *Friday the 13th* things."

Now she wondered if maybe she shouldn't have been so blasé about her non-involvement in those outings. Instead of seeing it as them respecting her lack of interest in being social, perhaps all along it'd been more about them not wanting to be around her that much. Maybe she *embarrassed* them.

She laughed bitterly, fresh tears shining in her eyes.

After staring at Julia's text for over a minute, she typed in a response that read, *Fuck that bitch.*

She stared at the words for nearly another full minute before erasing the message without sending it. It would only invite a discussion she didn't feel like having right now. She briefly considered denying she'd heard from Cassie before deciding not to reply at all.

She looked at her house and thought about going inside.

She also thought about backing out of the driveway and driving to a bar. Didn't matter which kind. Any place where she could sit and drink alone until she got shitfaced. It seemed unlikely, but if by some chance she did get hit on by some at least moderately decent-looking guy, maybe something would happen. Maybe she'd go back to his place and let him fuck her. That was something she almost never did, but maybe it'd be the right thing tonight. Maybe feeling anything other than pain wouldn't be such a bad thing, regardless of how fleeting.

In the end, she decided against it.

She didn't have the energy. Not only that, but she feared she'd wind up breaking down before she could even finish her first drink, and the prospect of allowing that to happen in public was beyond mortifying. No, she'd do what she always did when she was feeling blue. Turn out the lights and watch a horror movie in the dark while she got drunk. There was still a bottle of whiskey in one of the cupboards. That'd do the job just fine.

Allison got out of her car and walked stiffly toward the porch, feeling numb now in the aftermath of her sobbing fit. As she walked along the sidewalk, she heard Cassie's spiteful words in her head again. She couldn't understand the venom. Just last night, Cassie had seemed so supportive and caring, concerned about her well-being.

Even if they didn't hang out as much as she'd like, *that* part of their friendship had always seemed so solid.

How could she have been so goddamn wrong about that?

The absence of it made her feel hollow inside. Less than human. Just some empty cipher no normal person could ever truly care about.

A single tear slid down her face as she climbed up to her porch and unlocked the front door. It seemed she'd only thought to lock the regular lock upon leaving earlier, because the deadbolt was not engaged. She stepped into the foyer and closed the door. A weird prickling sensation on her arms made her breath catch in her throat. She'd heard nothing, but had a sense of being watched. Maybe it was a trick of her emotions. She was a wreck right now and perhaps her perceptive instincts were out of whack.

But she didn't think so.

She'd turned the deadbolt, but the key was still inside the lock. Her thumb and forefinger were still pinched around the key tab. There was an intruder in the house. Maybe the melting man from her dreams. Maybe a garden variety burglar or rapist. How she knew this without seeing or hearing anything she didn't know. She just *knew* it. The question now was did she have time to turn the deadbolt the other way, undo the bottom lock, and get the fuck out of her house before something terrible happened?

Don't think, just go.

She turned the deadbolt back the other way, the click it made as it retracted sounding conspicuously loud to her ears. Her hand was going to the doorknob when she sensed a presence rushing up behind her. This time there was undeniable aural proof—footsteps on the foyer tiles.

Strong hands roughly seized her and pulled her away from the door.

She screamed.

A hand clamped hard over her mouth, muffling the sound.

She squirmed in the intruder's grip and tried stamping at his instep, like she'd been taught for situations like this long ago. He shifted his stance as this was happening and her stomping foot only struck the floor. The next thing she felt was the sharp edge of a blade against her throat.

Then a voice spoke in her ear: "Knock it off or I'll slit your fucking throat."

Allison went silent and stopped squirming.

There was an exhalation of warm breath against her ear. "That's better. I don't want to hurt you, but I will if you don't fucking behave. Will you?"

Allison nodded.

Her heart was thudding painfully in her chest and her mind was going a million miles an hour. The terror she felt in those moments was immense. Despite the overwhelming darkness of her mood prior to entering the house, she now became intensely aware of how much she wanted to keep on living. Keep on existing and maybe someday even find better friends than the current ones who took her for granted so often. She knew there was nothing she wouldn't do to survive. Even as these realizations came crashing in, awareness of other things intruded.

The guy behind her was taller than she was by about a full head, judging from the way he was hunched over while holding onto her.

And there was something familiar about his voice.

It all came together in her head in a space of mere seconds.

Fuck. It's him.

The seeming impossibility of him tracking her down so quickly didn't even matter. He was here. That was the fucking reality. She could only accept it and start figuring out how to convince him not to kill her.

He dragged her into the living room and dropped her in the recliner next to the sofa.

Then he stepped backward and pointed the knife at her. "Where the fuck is it?"

It was a big butcher knife.

She recognized it as one of her own. It was one of a set and was normally in a wood block along with the others in the set on the kitchen counter.

She sighed. "What are you talking about?"

He made a sputtering sound of disbelief. "Don't give me that, bitch. That's some fucking nerve you've got, pretending like you don't know. Where's the tape?"

"I don't have it."

"Yeah, right."

She shrugged. "I did have it, yes, but I don't have it now. I'm serious. You can turn this place upside down. Look in every goddamn nook and cranny, but you won't find it."

He kept the knife pointed at her as he took a few steps back and turned his head this way and that, surveying the living room. His gaze lingered on the multiple bookcases lined with Blu-ray cases and VHS tapes.

"Stay right there." His eyes bulged as he made a threatening motion with the knife. "And stay fucking still. You move so much as a muscle, I'll be on you faster than a striking serpent."

Allison tried to stifle laughter, but wasn't entirely successful. "I'm sorry. Faster than a *what*?"

"You heard me."

"I know. I did. That's the problem."

He scowled. "You better not laugh at me. This isn't a fucking joke, bitch. Laugh again and you'll be fucking sorry."

Despite her terror—which was still considerable—her instinct was to verbally jab at him again, if only because it was so easy to get under his skin. This time, however, her common sense prevailed and she said nothing.

The guy moved over to the first of two bookcases stuffed full of VHS tapes, positioning himself in a way that allowed him to scan the tapes while also keeping an eye on her. She smirked as she watched his lips moving.

"What's your name, dude?"

He glanced at her. "Huh?"

She sighed. "Your real name. What is it? I know it's not Seth."

He went back to scanning the titles. "Figured that out, huh? I'm thinking you don't need to know my real name, in case I don't wind up killing your thieving ass."

"How about your first name?"

He looked at her again, his expression turning thoughtful. "I guess that'd be okay. It's a pretty fucking ordinary name."

"What is it?"

"Mark."

She frowned. "You're right. That is pretty goddamn ordinary."

He laughed. "Says the girl named fucking *Allison*."

She tilted her head, her frown deepening. "So you know my real name, too. Mind if I ask how you found me so fast? I thought I did a pretty good job of covering my tracks."

He shrugged. "You probably did. Wasn't my doing, to tell you the truth. My uncle found you. *Fuck*."

The frustration in his voice as he moved away from the bookcases was palpable. He was clearly on edge and desperate to recover the tape. Was he on edge enough to kill her when he arrived at the inevitable conclusion that the thing he wanted truly wasn't here?

She wasn't sure, but his edginess made her worry.

He went over to the Zenith and hit the eject button on the VCR, cursing again when the empty top-loader popped out.

She sighed. "Okay, so you've already checked the most obvious places. I guess you could keep going and search the whole fucking place, but you'll be wasting your time. The tape really isn't here."

She said these things with every ounce of sincerity she could muster, which was easy, given she was only telling him the plain truth of the matter.

Another scowl twisted his features as he came closer and started waving the knife around. "I wonder if you'd change your tune if I started cutting on you?"

Allison shook her head. "Nope. It'd be pointless to make something up, tell you the tape is here and not be able to produce it. For the millionth fucking time, it's *not* here." She let out a big breath as she stared into his eyes and made a decision. "But I can tell you where it is."

He stared silently at her a moment, studying her expression.

Belief began to dawn in his features. "Okay, fine. Where is it?"

She told him.

Then she rose from the recliner and approached him without fear. "I'll even go over there with you, help any way I can. That bitch betrayed me and I want my pound of flesh."

Mark frowned. "You serious?"

She nodded. "But before we go over there, I want you to take me into my bedroom and fuck me as hard as you can."

He opened his mouth, but said nothing, words apparently failing him. He hadn't expected this. How could he? She pushed the knife out of the way and moved even closer, until they were separated by only a few inches.

This wasn't calculated survival strategy.

It was only raw impulse.

Desire to feel something other than pain.

He didn't resist when she took him by the hand and led him out of the living room and down the hallway.

TWENTY-TWO

A LITTLE INTO THE SECOND of her back-to-back viewings of *Homecoming*, someone knocked on Cassie's door. This occurred at one of the quieter moments in the movie, with Jason observing nubile skinny dippers from behind some trees. A kill scene in which the masked mass murderer dispensed with an interloping hiker was mere moments away. Things would get loud again as the kill occurred and the film transitioned to a scene of adolescents involved in a mean-spirited game of dodgeball at the recently reopened Camp Crystal Lake.

She grabbed the remote and hit the pause button before the transition could happen. Her hope was that the person on the other side of the door had not heard the movie playing before knocking. If it was someone she knew, they'd know she was here, what with her bright red car being out there in the parking lot, but total silence from inside the apartment meant she could plausibly be in the shower or napping in her bedroom. She didn't want to see or talk to anyone right now, especially if this was Allison back for another round of histrionic begging.

A few moments passed as she held her breath and didn't move.

Then the knocking came again, more insistent this time.

And now a strident voice from the other side of the door: "Open up, Cassie. I know you're in there. I heard your fucking TV before you muted it or whatever."

Cassie sighed.

Not Allison. Thank God for that at least.

She dropped the remote on the coffee table and reluctantly went to the door. After undoing the multiple locks, she opened it and stared at her visitor. "What do you want?"

The look on Julia Laudner's face conveyed equal parts confusion and frustrated anger. "Are you serious right now? We were supposed to meet up over an hour ago. Remember?"

Cassie frowned.

She did remember. Now. In the midst of being so upset, however, she'd temporarily forgotten all about the plans she'd made with Julia the previous day.

"I'm sorry. I forgot."

Her friend was in a strapless green satin dress and heels. All dressed up for a night on the town.

"You forgot? How is that possible?"

Cassie sighed again and leaned against the edge of the open door. "Look, I'm really fucking sorry. This has been a really bad day. I would've let you know I wasn't up to going out, but I seriously forgot about our plans. I know that's shitty of me, but that's what happened."

Julia studied her face a moment before shrugging. "Okay, fine. Can I come in a minute, at least?"

Cassie suppressed the urge to groan.

She wasn't interested in having any kind of extended interaction with anyone, but a brief visit was pretty much obligatory after leaving her friend hanging like that. "Okay, but please only for a few minutes. I've got a terrible headache and want to go to bed soon."

She stepped back and opened the door wider, allowing Julia inside. The bit about the headache was a lie, but one with a purpose behind it. Mentioning it at the outset meant she had a seemingly legitimate reason for abruptly cutting the visit short at any point.

After closing the door, Cassie returned to her spot on the sofa, tucking her legs up beneath her.

Julia dropped her purse on the coffee table and glanced at the frozen image of Jason Voorhees on the TV screen. "There's my boy. Which one is this?"

Cassie stopped the movie and hit a button to rewind the tape.

"That's not as easy to answer as you'd think. I'll start it again and let you see for yourself."

Julia gave her a dubious look, then shrugged. "Weird, but whatever. You got anything alcoholic to drink?"

"There's a few beers in the fridge."

Julia glanced back at her as she started moving in that direction. "Want me to grab you one?"

"No."

Julia grunted. "I'll get you one anyway."

She went on into the kitchen and a moment later Cassie heard her open the refrigerator door. Bottles clinked as she removed them from the fridge. This was followed by the sound of caps being removed with an opener. Seconds later, she was back out in the living room with bottles in hand. After kicking off her shoes, she plopped down right next to Cassie on the sofa and leaned into her, resting her head on her shoulder.

Right after that, the tape finished rewinding.

Cassie aimed the remote at the VCR and started the movie again. Julia sipped her beer and snuggled closer, making a sound of blissful contentment. The physical contact was nice, even a bit calming after a day of emotional turmoil. Maybe this would turn into one of those occasional nights where they ended up getting physically intimate. That wouldn't be such a bad thing, either.

There was a moment where she believed Julia was right on the edge of initiating a makeout session when her attention was abruptly snared by the scene on the boat dock. "Hold on. Is that who I think it is?"

Cassie sighed. "Yes."

Julia pulled away from her and sat up straight, leaning forward on the edge of the sofa. "Holy shit. That's Ryan Laettner."

"I know."

Julia stared at the screen in open-mouthed mystification as the rest of the scene played out. Then she glanced at Cassie as the opening credits sequence started. "What the fuck is this movie?"

Cassie shrugged. "Like I said already, that's not an easy thing to answer. Best to sit back and watch."

So that's what they did.

Bracing herself for a barrage of difficult questions, Cassie started taking bigger gulps of her beer. She was more than mildly surprised when the expected interrogation failed to materialize. Julia's attention was locked on the TV and she said nothing as the next several scenes unfolded. It was clear she was completely enraptured by what she was seeing. That part of her reaction was, of course, no surprise at all.

Cassie shook her bottle. It was empty.

She got up and said, "I'm getting another beer. You need one yet?"

Julia shook her head, but did not otherwise reply.

She frowned and craned her head around as Cassie walked by in front of her. The same thing happened again a few moments later when Cassie returned with a fresh beer in hand. She sat down with a sigh and took a big gulp from the bottle while on the screen Jason was doing interesting things to a camp counselor's body with the blade of a long-handled shovel.

The extended conversational lull continued as she made her way through the second beer. She'd downed around half of it by the time she realized she had to pee. "Be right back."

She set the bottle on the coffee table and got up again.

Julia glanced up at her and spoke for the first time in a while. "Should I pause it?"

"Sure."

Julia grabbed the remote as Cassie walked out of the living room.

While sitting on the toilet in the hallway bathroom, Julia looked at her phone. There were no more messages or missed calls from Allison. In a way, this was a relief, but she also felt another of those nagging pangs of regret. She'd transgressed against her in an unforgivably egregious way, crossing many of the understood lines of friendship in a single fell swoop. She felt bad about it, even though she knew she wouldn't take it back. Maybe at some point down the line she could make it right, but that would probably be a while.

She finished up in the bathroom and walked back down the hallway to the living room. It was quiet out there, but that was to be expected with the movie on pause. Once she was back in the living room, however, she came to an abrupt stop and looked around.

Julia wasn't on the sofa.

She wasn't in the living room at all.

Cassie was confused for a moment, thinking maybe her friend had gone into the kitchen, but then her gaze went to the front door. In another fraction of a second, she would've missed it, but the door was in the process of being eased carefully into the frame. The way one would do it when trying to make no discernible noise.

Her gaze flicked to the coffee table.

Julia's purse was gone.

Her shoes weren't on the floor.

The TV screen displayed only white static.

Shit!

Cassie ran to the door and hauled it open, stepping outside in time to see Julia halfway across the landing to the staircase. The other woman glanced back and let out a squeal of dismay.

Cassie charged after Julia and caught up to her before she could start down the stairs, grabbing a handful of her long hair and yanking her backward. She shrieked in fright as Cassie spun her about and smashed her face against the wall. There was a crunching sound as cartilage yielded to unmoving brick. Blood spilled from the nostrils of Julia's crooked nose when she slumped down on the concrete landing. She turned and put her back to the wall, looking dazed as Cassie snatched up her purse and started rooting through it.

Julia whimpered. "You bitch. You broke my fucking nose."

Cassie plucked the videotape from the purse. "You're lucky you're getting off that easy." She tossed the purse to Julia. It hit her chest and fell into her lap. "Get the fuck out of here, bitch, and don't you dare come back."

She started moving toward the open door of her apartment.

Julia made a shrill sound of pained exertion as she lurched back to her feet and woozily turned toward Cassie. "Look what you did to me. I'll call the fucking cops on your ass. Put you in jail."

Cassie turned toward her as she reached the door.

She laughed. "Yeah, that's not gonna happen."

Julia sneered. "Oh, yeah. You just watch."

She started rummaging in her purse, probably looking for her phone.

Cassie came away from the door, making Julia squeal in fright again as she moved a few steps closer. "If you do this, it'll be some kind of minor assault charge. I have no record whatsoever, so I'll be bailed out in no time. And when that happens, I'll come for you." She kept coming closer as she talked, making Julia cringe and back away. "There'll be no one to stop me from getting to you. And you know what'll happen then?"

Julia whimpered and took another shaky backward step. "Wh-what?"

Cassie smiled. "I'll kill you. I'll slit your throat." She drew a fingertip across the hollow of her own throat. "Like that. Do you believe me?"

Julia sniffled and blinked back tears. "M-maybe ... maybe you could make me a cuh-copy ... of that tape for me."

Cassie's expression turned steely and unforgiving. "No. Fuck off." She went back into her apartment and slammed the door.

TWENTY-THREE

AFTER HE SHOT HIS LOAD inside her, the girl he'd come to Ohio to kill continued riding his still-stiff cock a while longer, bucking hard against him and screaming until at last it began to wilt. The bucking was so fierce it was making his back hurt. He was close to saying something about it when she finally started to wind down, shuddering in apparent orgasm. Then after that, she remained atop him a while longer, breathing hard, her face shiny with sweat. Without the makeup she'd caked on at the con, she was objectively average-looking, almost kind of plain, but right there in that moment, he truly believed she was the sexiest, most exciting woman he'd ever seen in his life.

At last, as her breathing finally started to even out again, she climbed off him and flopped down onto her back next to him.

Mark removed the hockey mask and turned his head to look at her. "You know, it's a little fucked-up that you made me wear this."

She snatched the mask away from him and held it in her hands, staring at it in a reverent way. "This is a film-used Jason Voorhees mask. I got it in a charity auction three years ago. Cost me a good chunk of my savings at the time."

"How much?"

She told him.

He whistled in amazement. "Jesus. What are you, rich?"

She shook her head and smiled in an off-kilter way. "No. I just really, really, really, *really* like *Friday the 13th*."

Mark looked around at the framed *Friday* posters adorning her bedroom walls. These weren't cheap Hobby Lobby frames. They were heavy-duty ones with thick glass. Museum-quality shit. Some of the posters hanging behind the glass were lined with creases from being folded and stored away decades ago. There were little nicks and holes around the edges. Not too hard to guess that these were all original release vintage posters. Nowhere near as valuable as that mask, but not cheap either.

"Wow. Damn. I guess you do."

She smirked. "And you didn't believe me when I told you at the con that I was the biggest *Friday* fan of all."

He grunted. "Well, you can stop trying to convince me, because there's no longer any goddamn doubt."

"Good."

They lay there in silence a while, staring up at the ceiling, lost in their individual thoughts.

Then Mark turned onto his side and reached out to delicately take a lock of her hair between his fingers. "I really like your hair, you know. The black tips. So cool. So sexy. Reminds me of the cute chick in part five."

She looked at him. "Tiffany Helm in *A New Beginning*. Yeah, that's intentional. Shit!" She thumped a fist against the mattress. "Goddammit. I should've put that Pseudo Echo song on while we were fucking. That would've been *perfect*."

Mark laughed.

Then his expression sobered. "Wouldn't it be funny if it turned out we were perfect for each other?"

She turned onto her side to face him more directly. "You were threatening to kill me a little while ago. Were you serious or just trying to scare me?"

He grimaced. "I don't want to kill you. Maybe I felt mad enough to when you stole the tape, but things have changed."

"Because we fucked again?"

He shrugged. "That's part of it. Sure. Of course it is. But it's more than that. I don't meet many girls like you, ones who are so into the same weird shit I am. Even when I do, they don't stay interested in me for long. This might surprise you, but I have trouble really connecting with people in general."

She shook her head. "That doesn't surprise me at all. I think we're a lot alike, actually. More than I realized when we met. I have a hard time connecting with people, too. The chick who stole my tape—"

Mark laughed. "*My* tape, you mean."

Allison rolled her eyes. "*Whatever*. Anyway, Cassie is the closest thing I've ever had to a truly close, intimate friend. I've got a few other friendly acquaintances, but nothing close to what I had with her. I always thought of us as platonic soulmates. And now that's over, I guess. It fucking sucks, because I don't think I'll ever have anything like that again."

"We could be like that, maybe."

Allison sighed. "Yeah. Maybe."

"You don't sound convinced."

Allison didn't reply to that immediately, staring into his eyes in a searching way before abruptly shifting around on the mattress and sitting up in the bed. She had a pensive, troubled air about her, and a faraway look in her eyes as she stared blankly at the wall opposite the foot of the bed. Mounted on the wall there was a framed poster for *The Final Chapter*, which included the famous tagline, *This is the one you've been screaming for.*

At last, she said, "We've got a lot to overcome, you and me, if we're ever gonna have a chance at being anything." There was sadness in the soft laughter that followed these words. "And that's got to be one of the biggest understatements anyone's ever made."

Watching her, he felt a stirring of something he hadn't felt in a long time, an emotional response to something in her softly uttered words. Not love, exactly. Even someone as broken as he was knew it was too early to really feel anything like that. But it nonetheless felt like a first tentative step in that direction. He wanted to make her feel better somehow, whether through words or deeds, only he didn't have the first clue what to say or do. It was a strange way to feel after being indifferent to the feelings of other people for so much of his life.

He thought about coming clean regarding the full truth of why his uncle had sent him here, that he'd been ordered to not only retrieve the tape but to kill her as well. Maybe by showing how open and unflinchingly honest he was willing to be, he would show himself as being worthy of her trust. Obviously the admission would necessarily be accompanied by strongly expressed reassurance of having no interest in actually killing her. That he'd only recently come to that conclusion—as in just the last several minutes—was irrelevant.

Of course, he couldn't be unflinchingly honest about *everything*.

He couldn't tell her about the hotel clerk in Virginia.

That would ruin everything, crush forever any hopes of the delicate thing taking cautious shape here from growing into something real. His head filled with an image of the clerk's face contorting with pain as he shoved the blade deep inside her belly. This time there was no excitement in reliving that moment, not even the slightest trace. He wished he could erase it from his mind, rewind time and make it so it'd never happened at all.

But that wasn't possible, of course.

No matter what he did with the rest of his life, nothing would change the fact that he was a murderer. Someone who'd killed an innocent person for no good reason other than purging the rage roiling inside him. Someone who, when you got down to it, was no better than the fucking scumbags who'd shot his parents.

Allison looked at him, frowning. "Something wrong?"

He sat up. "No."

"Liar."

He laughed. "Okay, yeah, that's bullshit. There's a lot wrong."

She stared intently at him a moment, her eyes focusing on particular parts of his face. The bruises and cuts. "Who did that to you?"

No clarification was necessary. He knew what she meant.

"My uncle."

"Your uncle beat the shit out of you?"

There was an uncomfortable tightening in his chest, a symptom of intense anxiety. He'd never told anyone about the things James Castleberry did to him sometimes. A significant part of his psyche rebelled against doing so even now, but a bigger part of him didn't want to hide from it anymore.

"Yes. He did." An unexpected welling of moisture in his eyes made him angry. "I know it's stupid. I'm a grown man now. I shouldn't let it keep happening. I should . . ."

He trailed off, at a loss as to what to say next.

A brief silence stretched out between them.

Then Allison sighed and said, "How long has this been going on? Talk to me about it. Tell me all the shit you've never been able to say."

Mark wept openly for a few moments.

Then he collected himself and began to talk at length on the subject.

TWENTY-FOUR

THE STORY MARK TOLD ALLISON was a genuinely sad and affecting tale of tragedy and horrific abuse over a long period of time. Listening to it, she felt empathy for him. No one should ever have to go through the terrible things he endured starting from a young age. She believed every word of it, too. There was too much raw emotion in his voice. She had a feeling he'd never been this unguarded and open with anyone about anything.

Despite feeling bad for him—or the kid he'd been at the start of his long ordeal, at least—she never lost sight of the harsh reality that this was the same guy who'd held a knife to her throat and threatened her life not even a half-hour earlier. Never forgot that he was an un-invited trespasser in her home. A stalker. A man who'd called her a bitch countless times, the word invested with palpable, hateful venom each time it passed through his lips.

He was a bad guy. Bottom line.

He was delusional to think there was any chance in hell of them having a relationship beyond this moment in time. Beyond the matter of the tape and however long it took to resolve that dilemma.

She would not allow herself to feel bad for using him, not after feeling that bite of sharp steel against her vulnerable flesh. There was no doubt in her mind this guy was fully capable of killing her under the right circumstances. Offering herself to him physically was trauma-infused instinct only, a desperate and self-destructive attempt at blunting her own emotional pain, akin to deliberately stepping out untethered onto a skyscraper ledge. Just to feel her life hanging in the balance, a walk along the edge of oblivion, daring fate to take her. While she'd done it with no conscious intent of manipulating him, she saw now she had a chance at exploiting the weaknesses he'd revealed in the wake of their interlude of intimacy.

But she'd have to proceed with caution.

And be careful about the things she said to him.

A period of slightly awkward silence ensued after he was done talking.

Allison cleared her throat. "There's something I don't understand. Why does your uncle care so much about you getting that tape back? I mean, I get you would want it, but what is it to him?"

He sighed. "That's another complicated story. It has to do with how I got the tape in the first place."

Allison flashed back to the wild theory she'd laid out for Cassie last night. That'd just been a case of her mind creatively hypothesizing, working to make sense of the inexplicable. In the absence of any logical explanation for the tape's existence, she'd even sort of halfway believed her theory last night, though in the light of day she'd been less sure.

Well, here was her chance to find out whether there was anything to it.

Maybe.

"Is it from another world?"

The look of wide-eyed shock on his face was so pronounced it was almost comical. "What the . . . how did you know that?"

She studied the look on his face a moment longer. There was nothing in it that suggested he was playing with her or going along with an absurd joke.

She shrugged. "It was just an idea I had when I was trying to figure out how such an impossible thing could exist. It's true, isn't it? It's not from here."

Mark ran a hand through his hair, shaking his head in amazement. "Christ. Yeah, it's from an alternate reality."

"So how did it get here?"

"The Visitor."

Allison frowned. "The what?"

A pained look creased his features. "You got anything strong to drink in this house? Whiskey or something? Because this part of it won't be easy, for me to talk about or for you to hear."

Allison almost laughed.

As if any of this had been easy so far.

Instead of saying that, she rolled out of bed and started pulling on her clothes.

Mark looked confused. "What are you doing?"

"Getting dressed so we can go get a drink somewhere. I know a place where we can get a quiet table" She pulled on her bra and adjusted it slightly, then scooped her shirt off the floor. "Come on, hurry. I could use a drink, too, and I really want to get out of the house. The sooner you can tell me about the rest of this, the sooner we can head on over to Cassie's and get that fucking tape back."

Mark smiled. "Works for me."

He got out of bed and reached for his clothes.

Less than five minutes later, they were in her car and driving away.

She had conflicted feelings as she steered them through the streets of Hilliard. There was power in being the one behind the wheel. She could take them anywhere, even right up to the doors of the police station. Depending on how she approached the building, she could probably get into the parking lot before he realized anything was amiss. And what could he do when he did figure it out? Grab the wheel and try to make her crash? It would be about the only option he'd have at that point. He didn't have a gun. The pilfered knife had been left behind at her house. Maybe when she stopped the car, he could jump out and make a run for it, but how far could he get with the police right there?

The notion was a tempting one. Shedding herself of this guy would at least temporarily guarantee her personal safety. It surprised her how he'd acquiesced so easily to letting her drive. Did he even understand how vulnerable surrendering that element of control made him? She wasn't sure it'd even entered his mind as a consideration. They'd had sex and exchanged personal intimacies, a sharing of secrets that probably resulted in him trusting her more than he otherwise would. He might see them as a real team now, two people united toward a common goal, with a deeper level of romance a possibility for the future should things work out.

If he was truly that gullible, it gave her a big advantage over him in a lot of ways.

The other side of it was just as complex. While she didn't relish prolonging their time together, there was more she needed to know about the tape. More she needed to know about The Visitor, whoever or whatever that was. Perhaps there might yet be a way to reclaim the tape—or at least a copy of it—and then permanently separate herself from Mark in some diplomatic fashion that spared his feelings. She had her doubts on that count, though. He'd displayed so much rage at first. Rage so intense she suspected it must always be lurking beneath the surface, always in danger of being triggered.

It was one hell of a thorny dilemma all the way around.

She pulled to a stop at an intersection, waiting for the light to change. Here already was a moment of crucial decision. A turn to the right would take her in the direction of the police department, though it would still be miles away. Her fingers flexed around the steering wheel as she watched the light and thought about it.

"Nervous?"

She flinched at the sound of his voice. It was the first thing he'd said in several minutes. She summoned a smile as she glanced at him. "I'm pretty anxious, I guess. Things are a little better now, but it's been a shit day. I could really use that drink. Or a few of them."

He nodded. "Yeah. I hear that." He sniffed at the air in a pointed way. "Funny thing. First time I ever saw you, you were inhaling a cigarette. But your car doesn't reek of cigarette smoke. Your house didn't either."

She grunted. "I pretty much only smoke at cons. It's a nerves thing. Makes me less anxious about being around so many people."

"You're anxious a lot, it seems."

She smirked. "No shit."

The light turned green.

She hesitated only a moment longer before putting her foot to the gas and driving straight through the intersection. Though it was technically still possible to wend her way back around in the direction of the police department by taking some additional turns up ahead, she knew she would not do that. The decision was made. She would see this through. There was a feeling of the inevitable in this, as if a part of her had known all along this was how it would be.

The bar she had in mind was only another couple miles away. At the next intersection, she took a left turn and after getting up to around the posted speed limit, she glanced at the rearview mirror.

And then she screamed.

THE UNSEEN

The man with the melting face was in the backseat, staring back at her in the mirror.

TWENTY-FIVE

AFTER FLEEING THE BUILDING WHERE Cassie lived, Julia Laudner drove aimlessly through the streets of Hilliard. Her path was a circuitous one, never traveling too far afield from the site of the violent incident. At first she drove with no clear intent, keeping the windows down and feeling the rush of incoming air against her face. She thought about going to the police to report the assault, but each time she considered this possibility she was dissuaded by the memory of Cassie's threats. Threats she took seriously. Julia had never heard her talk like that before, with such a vile, evil tone in her voice. It hurt her to even think about it.

She also considered a trip to the ER or one of those walk-in clinics. Her nose was still out of alignment and hurt so bad it had her perpetually on the edge of crying. There was a bottle of OxyContin in her purse. She reached over to the passenger seat and dug around in the purse until she found the vial. After popping off the non-child proof top of the illegally purchased pills, she knocked back two of them and took her hands off the steering wheel long enough to attempt putting the top back on.

Unfortunately, as soon as her hands came clear of the wheel, her Volvo veered across the center line, forcing her to drop the vial and grab hold of the wheel again in order to avoid a head-on collision with oncoming traffic. As she wrenched the Volvo back into its proper lane, the vial fell into the footwell and rolled around, spilling pills everywhere.

Julia screamed in frustration and resurgent anger.

Horns honked all around her as the Volvo swerved again. She waved a middle finger around and screamed some more. A few passing motorists returned the gesture, which did nothing to dull her already burning rage. Breathing hard through clenched teeth, she jerked the Volvo over into the right lane as soon as an opening appeared. She glanced ahead and spied a fast-food restaurant coming up on the right. On impulse, she turned into the lot and parked in one of the empty spaces away from the building. The spot she picked was at the far end of the lot, with multiple spaces between her and the next closest car.

She made no attempt to scoop up the pills she'd dropped. That wasn't why she'd stopped. Her emotions were running out of control and she needed to calm down before getting back out in traffic. Also in her purse was a half-pint bottle of pineapple vodka. Unopened. She always kept one on her for maintenance drinking. That was probably symptomatic of being a raging alcoholic, but in that moment she didn't give one shit. In truth, she never gave much of a damn. She loved alcohol. It was a fucking miracle elixir that took the edge off life. Without it, existence would be intolerable.

After digging out the bottle, she tore off the seal, removed the cap, and took a big gulp, sighing as the liquid slid smoothly down her throat. She took another gulp right after that and then another. Only then could she finally feel her overstimulated nerves start to settle.

She looked at the rearview mirror and grimaced when she saw her bloody visage.

God, I'm ugly now. That fucking bitch.

She gave the old car's mirror an angry twist, angling it so she would not again catch sight of herself before getting back out on the road. Leaning back in her seat, she gulped more vodka and tried again to will herself back toward a state of calmness. The effort was only semi-successful.

Her thoughts, however, returned to the events that precipitated the shitty course the day had taken. Everything was fine until Cassie started that movie and then it was as if she became hypnotized by it. No, it was more than that. She felt changed by it. Not in a grotesquely physical way as in *Videodrome*, but on a cerebral level. The wiring of her brain felt altered. The more of the movie she saw, the more she became a creature that needed to possess the movie. A strange, all-encompassing desire she could not explain, but her lack of under-standing made it no less real. When Cassie went into the bathroom, she truly felt as if she had no choice but to seize the opportunity and run off with the tape.

Unfortunately, she hadn't moved fast enough and now here she was.

Ugly.

Disfigured.

No longer even friends with her former favorite person in the world.

She reached up and angled the mirror back into its proper posi-tion. This time when she looked at herself she didn't flinch or look away. She gave her image a prolonged appraisal. A doctor could reset her nose and maybe months down the line she might look close to her old, undamaged self. Beautiful again.

But there'd be no more of those occasional intimate nights with Cassie.

And she'd definitely never see that impossible *Friday the 13th* movie again.

Unless she took action.

Which she had the means to do.

She just needed the will.

After staring at herself a moment longer, she came to a decision, and when she did, a sense of beautiful, restorative peace came over her. A smile tugged at the edges of her mouth. She would have what she wanted.

What she *needed*.

She heaved a breath and backed the Volvo out of the parking space.

After easing back into traffic, she drove in a calmer fashion. The OxyContin was starting to kick in, along with the booze. She felt like she was floating on a cloud as she drove down the street and eventu-ally got herself turned back in the direction of Cassie's apartment building.

Around ten minutes later, she pulled into the building's small parking lot and parked in a space at the curb. Cassie's red Versa was parked in a corner space at the back of the lot, as it nearly always was when she was here. She had mixed feelings about that. Executing her plan would be a lot easier with Cassie gone, but it ultimately didn't matter. She was prepared to deal with any eventualities. That tape would be hers within a few minutes and nothing would stand in the way of that.

Before getting out, she used some wipes from her purse to gently clean the blood from her face. Each touch brought another sting of pain, but she needed to make herself semi-presentable when she knocked on Norman Atwood's door. Old Norm was the live-in maintenance man here. He had one of the bottom floor units. The tubby and garrulous dude was in late middle-age and liked to flirt a bit with younger ladies. They had a friendly little rapport, the two of them. Perhaps she could use that to her advantage. If it worked, great. If not, again, she was ready to do whatever necessary to achieve her goal.

Her face looked as good as it was going to minus expert medical attention. She considered attempting to reset her crooked nose herself, but abandoned the idea the instant she gripped it, jerking her fingers away and biting back a shrill scream of pain.

She grabbed her purse and got out of the Volvo.

Seconds later, she stood in front of Norm's door.

She knocked and moved back a step, sliding a hand inside her purse. The hand stayed there while she waited for Norm to come to his door, which didn't take very long. Heavy footsteps approached from the other side, followed by the sound of the deadbolt retracting.

The door opened and Norm peered out at her, a wary expression on his face that was unlike him. "Miss Julie. What brings you to my door?"

Miss Julie was what he always called her. No one else in her life called her Julie. She hated being called that and was never shy about letting people know it. Her name was Julia and that was how she expected people to address her. Old Norm was the only person in recent history who'd gotten a pass from her where that was concerned. Mostly because he was older and she didn't expect much in the way of social graces from geezers.

She considered trying to flash him her usual bright smile, but refrained, knowing the attempt would look ghoulish now, given the altered configuration of her face. "Hey, Norm. I hate to bother you, but I left something up in Cassie's place. Something important. Normally I'd wait to get it back some other time, but I kind of need it now."

He frowned. "Oh. That's too bad, but, uh . . . what does this have to do with me? Why don't you go knock on her door?"

She sighed. "Well, that's the thing. I don't think she'd hear me. She was drinking a lot earlier. And, well . . . I shouldn't tell you this, it's private business, really, but she took some pills, too. I'm pretty sure she's dead to the world right now."

Norm shrugged. "I still don't see what this has to do with me."

Julia sighed again, more heavily this time, and edged a little closer. The proximity made him nervous. She could see that in the widening of his eyes. Her face might be out-of-whack, but her body still looked nice in the shimmery satin dress. He couldn't help glancing quickly at the exposed tops of her breasts.

"Come on, Norm, you know what I'm after. I know you've got a skeleton key for all the other units. You know, for when you gotta do maintenance stuff when the residents are out." She smirked and leaned closer, giving him an even better look at the goods. "Or for when you just feel like snooping around in their shit."

His expression changed then, shifting to convey his indignation. "I'd never do anything like that."

She laughed. "Bullshit. I bet you go up there and paw through Cassie's undies every chance you get. Tell me the truth. Do you sniff them?" She laughed again. "Take some as souvenirs, maybe?"

Norm shook his head, a disgusted look on his face. "I don't know what's gotten into you, Miss Julie, but you need to leave now. I wasn't going to say anything, but I heard the two of you screaming at each other a little while ago. I heard the fight. I almost called 911. Maybe I should've."

The look of teasing amusement vanished from her face.

She took her hand out of the purse and showed him the .38. The revolver was for personal protection. That was her original intent in purchasing the weapon, anyway. As a single, attractive woman, she often found herself in situations where she might be vulnerable to a predator. Having the gun made her feel safer. She'd only fired it once since buying it nearly a year ago. That was during her one and only training lesson at a shooting range. She'd been about halfway convinced she'd never fire it again.

Norm's mouth dropped open when he saw the gun.

He looked terrified.

Good.

She backed him into his apartment and closed the door.

129

THE UNSEEN

Just a few minutes later, the sound of a muffled gunshot emanated from the apartment.

TWENTY-SIX

A SECOND SCREAM FOLLOWED RIGHT on the heels of the first as Allison surrendered to pure terror. Her hands came away from the steering wheel, but her foot remained on the gas pedal, causing the car to veer sharply to the right, directly toward a line of cars parked at the curb.

Mark reached over and grabbed hold of the steering wheel, giving it a hard twist in time to avoid a crash. "Hit the brake! *Allison!*"

He had no idea what was causing her to freak out in such dramatic fashion, but he did know they'd crash soon if he couldn't snap her out of it. A crash of any significance—basically, anything more serious than a minor fender bender—would bring cops to the scene.

And that was something he definitely didn't want.

He screamed at her again, but her foot remained pressed to the gas. His hand was still on the wheel, twitching this way and that as he awkwardly guided them around other vehicles, narrowly avoiding scraping against a few of them. Something had to be done and soon. This was a desperate measures moment if ever there'd been one. He didn't want to have to hit her, but maybe he could shake her out of it.

He was starting to reach for her when she abruptly took her foot off the gas. She blinked rapidly and looked around, her bottom lip trembling. Then she pushed his hand away and grabbed hold of the wheel again, reasserting control of the vehicle. "I need to stop. Like, now."

He laughed in a humorless way, shaking his head. "Yeah, okay. That'd probably be a great fucking idea."

Moments later, she steered the Chevy Cruze into a gas station parking lot and pulled up to one of the gas pumps. She put the car in park, unbuckled her seatbelt, threw open the door on her side, and got out. He watched her wobble over to the trash can next to the pump. When she got there, she promptly bent over and vomited into the vaguely octagonal hole at the top of the can. As she did this, she pushed her hair away from her face, allowing him to see her mouth working as she struggled not to puke again. A thin line of drool trailed from one corner of her mouth and she wiped it away with the back of a hand.

He got out of the car and approached her without getting too close, wary of spooking her. "You okay?"

She made a whimpering sound and shuddered, then glanced at him and nodded in a tentative way that did not inspire full confidence. "Just give me a fuckin' minute, okay?"

He nodded. "Take as long as you need."

His words, however, did not reflect his true feelings.

If anything, the incident made him even more acutely aware of the urgent need to retrieve the tape as soon as possible. He still wasn't certain what had frightened her so badly, but he was sure there was nothing random about it. This was connected in some way with the overarching matter of the tape. He could even possibly hazard a guess as to what that was, but he wasn't ready to verbalize it yet.

He needed to hear her say it first.

At last, she stood up straight and moved away from the trash can. Instead of approaching him, however, she veered away and moved toward the driver's side of the car. Her approach was tentative, strongly suggestive of a terror that lingered still. She moved past the open door, not even glancing in at the front seat. Her breathing quickened as she leaned her torso forward and peered into the back of the car, apprehension obvious in her quivering expression.

She stood motionless for a few moments.

Then she moved closer and peered in for a while longer

Finally, she stood erect again and looked at him over the roof of the car. "He's gone. The man with the melting face is gone."

She sniffled, trembling in visible relief.

Mark sighed.

Fuck.

He circled around to the other side of the car, approaching her in the same tentative way. This time she didn't flinch or tell him to back off. He moved closer still, until they were almost in touching range. "It's okay," he told her, striving for a soothing tone. "You saw The Visitor. I'm sorry, I should've insisted on telling you more before we left your house. The thing you saw isn't from this world. Whether it's a man or something else, I don't know, but his face not only looks like it's melting, sometimes it's a blur, like a film image going in and out of focus. That's because The Visitor, as my uncle called him, rarely comes fully into this reality. He glides *between* realities, like an inter-dimensional surfer."

Allison's brow furrowed. "And you know these things because your uncle told you about them? Not this Visitor himself?"

Mark shook his head. "The Visitor doesn't communicate like that. Not with words. It's more of a mental thing, but it can only happen when he attaches himself to a person. Like a parasite." The sudden look of alarm on her face prompted another shake of his head. "No, he's not attached to you. Not yet."

"How do you know that?"

He tapped a finger against his temple. "Because I can still feel him in here. I know what it feels like. And I'd know what it felt like if he was suddenly gone, no longer attached. Attachment, by the way, only happens with willingness, at least at the start. Like an invitation."

Her lip curled and she arched an eyebrow in a way that suggested appalled disbelief. "And you did that? Invited him in? Why?"

He grimaced. "Because I was a dumb kid. My uncle made me think that hosting The Visitor would be a dream come true, like having my own personal Santa Claus always there to give me the things I wanted. Special things that shouldn't exist. Things no one else could have. For me, that meant movies. For someone else, it might be rare coins or books or whatever. That all depends on the person."

As he told her these things, his gaze roved around. A heavyset woman at the next pump over was staring at them with an odd, hard-to-read look on her doughy face. He realized the woman was less than ten feet away, possibly close enough to have heard every word he'd said, all of which would sound like pure insanity to her. Her attention stirred his anger, but he tried not to let it show, knowing it wouldn't be wise to make her even more wary or suspicious. She might be one of those overbearing busybodies, always alert for any opportunity to call the cops on some strangers.

The world was fucking full of them these days.

He gave her a smile and a nod.

Then he looked at Allison, lowering his voice as he said, "We should continue this conversation in the car."

She shook her head in an emphatic way. "Oh, hell no. That's where I saw that creepy fucker."

Mark sighed. "Doesn't matter. You might see him anywhere. In the car. In your house. Walking down the fucking street. Besides, you can't abandon your car here. You know that. If it makes you feel any easier about things, I'll drive. I'm used to the fucker showing himself to me at random times. I don't like it much either, but I can handle it."

She thought about that a moment before shaking her head again, albeit in a less alarmed way this time. "No, I'll do it. Let's get out of here."

Before he could reply, she moved past him and slid into the car, situating herself behind the wheel again. He watched her give the rearview mirror a long appraisal. Then she looked at him with an impatient look on her face. "You getting in or not?"

He nodded. "Yeah."

She shooed him out of the way and pulled her door shut.

After a moment's hesitation, he went around to the other side and got in next to her.

Mark breathed a sigh of relief as Allison pulled away from the pump and steered them back out into traffic, leaving behind the nosy heavyset woman, who'd never stopped staring at them.

Allison glanced at him. "I'm thinking we should skip that drink and head straight to Cassie's place."

That, too, came as a massive relief.

He nodded. "That's probably for the best."

Allison stopped at an intersection and looked at him again. "So if The Visitor isn't attached to me, why am I seeing him? Why has he come to me in my dreams?"

Mark glanced at her, a look of reproval on his face. "Come on, you know why. It's because you took the tape. Took his gift, something intended only for me. My uncle calls that opening a channel in the ether. By doing that, you led him straight to your door, so to speak. And you're seeing him because now he's interested in you. He's studying you."

Allison shifted in her seat and shivered. "Ugh."

She looked creeped out.

Good. She should be.

They drove through the intersection.

Allison's fidgety demeanor made it clear she remained deeply unsettled by what he'd told her. "If you get the tape back, will he leave me alone? I'm not in danger of that thing attaching itself to me the way it did to you?"

Mark shook his head. "Absolutely not. Like I said, you have to be willing. And The Visitor has to be interested. It's a mutual thing. It can harass you, but unless you let it in, it'll eventually go away."

Allison did not respond to that.

They drove in silence for another few blocks.

In another few minutes, Allison slowed the Chevy Cruze to a near crawl, hit her blinker light, and took a right turn down a side street. To their immediate left was a small apartment building. Looked like just four units with a breezeway in the middle.

Allison hit her blinker again and pulled into the small lot out front of the building. Right after that, she pulled into an empty space next to an older-looking Volvo with a tan paint job.

After cutting the engine, she turned her head and glanced at the Volvo. "That's my other friend's car. Julia. Her being here might make this easier."

"How?"

Allison opened her door. "Calming influence. They've got a weird dynamic, those two. Sometimes I think they're sort of halfway in love with each other. Cassie might not be so unreasonable with her around."

Mark grunted. "Let's hope you're right."

He opened his door and within another few seconds they were up on the sidewalk and headed toward the breezeway.

TWENTY-SEVEN

ALLISON WAS HAVING MORE OF those mixed feelings as she led Mark toward the steps leading up to the breezeway's second floor landing. While the urgency of reclaiming the tape hadn't faded for her, she did feel an intense level of reluctance about leading this sketchy guy right to her friend's door. That they could now be more accurately described as former friends made no difference. Bringing him here still felt wrong, like a shitty thing to do, yet she felt she had no better option. Circumstances had boxed her into a corner. The most she could hope for was to mitigate the level of shittiness as best she could, while still getting that tape back.

Then, hopefully, she could convince Mark to let her make a copy before he returned to wherever the hell he was really from with the original. At this point, she would feel no hesitation in using sex to again influence his feelings on the matter, albeit in a more deliberate way this time.

She'd gone four steps up the staircase when the shouting started from somewhere above her. Female voices. No question to whom they belonged. That was worrisome. She'd never heard her friends fight like that. Not even *close* to anything like that. She went up another step and that was when the first shot rang out. The sound was so startling she staggered and had to grip the rail to keep from tumbling back down the stairs.

Someone up there screamed.

Then came three more booming gunshots in quick succession.

Allison's grip tightened around the rail as her whole body began to tremble. She dimly perceived a sound of retreating footsteps and turned her head to see Mark standing out on the sidewalk. Until a moment ago, he'd been right behind her, but now he was breathing hard and looking at her with wide, terrified eyes. She thought of what he'd told her about how his parents died. Unexpectedly hearing gunshots at close range was undoubtedly triggering a debilitating episode of PTSD.

The smart thing to do would be to follow him back down the stairs, hop in her car, and drive away from here at high speed. She wanted that tape back more than anything, but did she want to die for it?

Some moments passed as she hesitated.

Mark started mouthing words at her, silently urging her to come on and flee with him. As a few more moments passed with no further violent sounds emerging from upstairs, however, she let out a breath and loosened her grip on the rail.

Then she turned her head and stared up the steps.

Mark spoke in an alarmed stage whisper: "Allison, don't."

But she didn't respond.

She let go of the rail and started up the stairs.

Mark continued making sounds of distress, but she ignored them.

She was shaking even harder as she arrived at the top of the stairs and saw that Cassie's door was standing partly open. Someone inside the apartment was weeping quietly. She couldn't tell who it was, but the lack of any other sound from in there filled her with dread. There was no benign way of explaining away those gunshots. Someone in there was almost certainly dead.

One of her friends.

She had tears of her own brimming in her eyes as she stepped up onto the landing and took the first few tentative steps toward that open door. Her heart thudded like a sledgehammer in her chest as second thoughts assailed her. This was a volatile situation filled with unknowns. If she stuck her head inside that door, she might find herself the next one on the wrong side of a bullet.

An alarmed inner voice screamed at her to turn and run.

Instead, she took another steadying breath and took a few more steps toward the door. The weeping from inside continued. She still couldn't tell who was making the sound. Her nose picked up a slightly acrid smell she supposed was gunpowder, an odor that brought home the grim reality of what had transpired. A part of her mind was still telling her to stop moving forward, but there was a momentum to what she was doing that could not be stopped, not until she saw for herself what had happened.

Until she saw who was dead.

The door was only a few feet away now.

Another step or two and she'd be able to reach out and touch the frame.

She took one more step and stopped, her hands curling into trembling fists while her heart continued to thud away so loudly it was like thunder in her ears.

Then a voice spoke in a near monotone: "I can hear you breathing out there. Might as well come on in."

Allison sniffled and wiped away tears.

Cassie.

She steeled her nerves as best she could and moved into the open doorway. A gasp of shock leapt from her mouth when she saw Julia's crumpled form on Cassie's living room floor. There was a lot of blood and some pink tissue that might be bits of brain or bloody bone fragments. Holes in her face and at the side of her head. A bigger exit wound at the back of her head. It hurt to see the ruin of someone who'd been so beautiful.

Someone who'd been her friend.

Cassie sat on the arm of her sofa.

The gun—a revolver of some kind—was still in her hand, aimed now at Allison's midsection. "Come in and close the door. Lock it, too."

One more impulse to make a break for it and flee came and went.

Allison entered the spacious apartment, closing and locking the door behind her, just as she'd been told.

She moved a few cautious steps deeper into the apartment and stopped. "Since when do you have a gun? I thought you hated them."

Cassie's face was streaked with tears, but she was no longer openly weeping. "It's not mine. I never fired a gun in my life until now."

"Then where did it come from?"

Cassie smirked. "Use your head, Allison. It didn't materialize out of fucking nowhere. It's Julia's gun. Check this out. She let herself in with some kind of goddamn skeleton key. Then she came at me with the gun, making threats. She came too close and I made a grab for the gun. She dropped it and we wrestled for it. I won. Obviously."

Allison shook her head, her features arranged in a look of grim, horrified disbelief. "And you shot her? You didn't make her leave or call the cops. Why?"

Cassie stared at her a moment, her face hardening with anger.

Then she got to her feet and came at Allison fast.

There was nowhere to go, no place to hide or retreat.

Cassie clamped a hand around her throat and drove her backward, pressing her up against the wall. Still warm from being fired, the muzzle of the gun pressed against her face. "How dare you ask me that fucking question. You're the one who set all this in motion, you bitch. You did it when you took the fucking tape. There's something wrong with it. Something that gets into your head and fucks with it. It happened to me and it happened to Julia when I let her watch it." Tears were streaming from her eyes again. "It doesn't belong here. It shouldn't exist. You fucked with things you weren't meant to fuck with and now look at us. Our beautiful little circle is broken and it's not ever gonna be put back together."

Allison's vision blurred as a strangled sob emerged from her mouth. "I'm so sorry."

Cassie laughed bitterly. "Save it. Fuck your apology." She tapped Allison's cheek with the barrel of the gun. "One bullet left. Who gets it? Me or you? It should be you."

Allison mewled and clawed at the wall behind her.

Cassie was right. She deserved it.

She whimpered. "Do it. Just do it. Nobody loves me. I'm worthless. I've always been worthless. Kill me. Please kill me."

Cassie laughed. "You're not getting off that easy, you fucking cunt."

She let go of Allison's throat and backed off.

She smiled.

Then she put the barrel of the gun in her mouth and pulled the trigger. A red mist sprayed outward from the back of her head and her body dropped like a rock to the floor.

Allison gagged as she pushed away from the wall and gaped in disbelieving horror at the carnage around her. The lifeless bodies of her only friends in the world taunted her, mocked her. They hadn't been perfect friends, not always, but was there really any such thing?

Regardless, they'd been the only real ones in her life.

And now they were fucking *gone*.

Irretrievably. Forever.

The loss was of a magnitude impossible to comprehend. She didn't know if she'd ever be able to understand it.

She remained frozen in numb disbelief an indeterminate time longer. Maybe around a minute. She might have stayed that way much longer, if not for hearing the first faint sounds of sirens in the distance. While she couldn't know for sure they were headed here, it seemed a safe assumption.

Stepping carefully around the bodies, she went to Cassie's VCR and jabbed at the eject button. Out popped a tape. It was the one she expected to see. She set it aside and frantically hunted for Cassie's phone. It took her maybe thirty seconds, but it felt like forever. With trembling fingers, she entered the unlock code, found her chat log with Cassie, and deleted it. No time to search her messages with other people. Allison would just have to hope her dead friend made no mention of the tape in any of them. After returning the phone to Cassie's purse, she grabbed the tape and hurried out of the apartment, then down the stairs.

Mark was nowhere in sight.

The sirens were getting louder and closer.

She hurried to her car and yanked open the door, leaned in, and stuffed the tape into her glovebox. Backing out of the car, she threw the door shut and returned tiredly to the staircase.

She sat on one of the lower steps and waited.

TWENTY-EIGHT

LAID OUT ON A TABLE in the detached garage outside his house were various parts of a 1970 Corvette's engine. With a grimy rag in his hand, James Castleberry approached the table and stared at the parts, trying to think in his usual methodical way about where he needed to go next in this early stage of the engine reassembly.

This was usually easy, instinctive stuff, work of a type he'd done so much of over so many years it'd become second nature. He worked with the practiced precision and smooth certainty of a skilled craftsman, his hands knowing what to do with him barely having to think of it. The large yard out back of his rural property was filled with various automotive projects in progress, as well as the rusted husks of relics that would never be driven again. He kept the husks around because they were often good for scavenging parts. Some of the project cars he'd purchased from auctions or rescued from junk-yards. Others had rolled off assembly lines in other worlds, special models never produced in this reality. The bitch of that was he could never drive them anywhere other than around his own property. A few other cars once belonged to people who'd perished out here. Missing people who'd never be seen again.

These were the twin passions of his life.

Cars and murder.

Being a good bit older now, he was more or less retired from the recreational murder game, but he still liked to work on automobiles, using stray bits from jalopies to build back a beautiful piece of Detroit muscle and steel.

He loved nothing more than that.

But lately he was having trouble concentrating.

Almost a full week had gone by without hearing so much as a peep from his brainless nephew. The kid was dumb as a box of rusty nails, but for much of the boy's life James had been able to count on him doing as he was told. The reason was fear. Teaching him the importance of absolute and unwavering obedience was something he'd accomplished over a period of years with his fists and a thick leather strap. Until the incident at the horror convention, the boy had never shown signs of forgetting his lessons, but now it seemed he was off the rails, perhaps going through a belated rebellious period. He was due for a long period of tough correction, it seemed. Some months chained up in the basement of his uncle's house would hopefully set him straight.

For that to happen, though, he'd first have to come back to Illinois.

Unfortunately, James currently had no idea where the dumb little cocksucker might be. The GPS tracker he'd installed on the kid's Mustang had either been removed or was malfunctioning. He hadn't been able to get a signal from it in days.

He muttered a curse and tossed the dirty rag down on the table. The frustration of it all was getting to him. He was starting to wonder if it'd been worth it all those years ago, when he'd murdered the boy's parents and made it look like a botched robbery. The goal he had in mind back then was clear in his head from the start. He wanted to rid himself of The Visitor, to halt the thing's slow, prolonged consumption of his mind and soul. His fear at the time was he'd soon become something other than human if he allowed it to go on much longer. Taking young Mark under his wing gave him the perfect opportunity to shape a malleable and vulnerable mind, to direct him toward his sacrificial purpose.

For a long time, things seemed to have worked out perfectly.

But now Mark was fucking up.

He was forgetting the rules. The gifts were not to be shared. *Ever.* The farther away they got from their intended recipient, the more dangerous they became. The Visitor didn't like that. The instability.

And now James was worried the dimwit would wind up getting himself killed. He didn't give one shit about the kid as a human being, but as long as he was alive, James himself would remain safe.

If Mark died, The Visitor would return to its previous host.

James gritted his teeth, shaking with rage and frustration.

Me.

Fucking thing will come back to ruin the rest of my goddamn life.

He slammed the base of a fist against the table, making engine components rattle.

A loud thump made his head snap toward the open door of the garage. He stared in confusion at the small form standing just inside the door.

Then he laughed.

"Who the fuck are you supposed to be?"

The girl was slender and maybe a couple inches over five feet tall. A slight thing. She wore black leggings, a plain black t-shirt, and black boots. Her face was hidden by an old-fashioned hockey mask. That last part puzzled him until he realized it was a replica of the type worn by the killer in one of those dumb slasher movies Mark liked. Gripped in her right hand was a machete. He saw now she'd knocked it against the garage door frame, cutting a notch in the wood.

Now she held the machete in front of her and moved a slow step closer.

James tilted his head, squinting at her.

Still more puzzled than worried.

He smirked. "Am I supposed to be afraid of you?"

She came another step closer, waving the machete slowly back and forth.

James frowned.

He reached toward the table and picked up a heavy wrench, hefting it and slapping it against his palm. "Are you some friend of Mark's? Where is that worthless sack of shit?"

The girl said nothing and came another step closer.

James sneered. "Yeah, keep on comin', bitch. I don't even care who you are. Come closer. I'll break you in half and fuck your corpse. Won't be a first for me."

He laughed.

The girl came another step closer.

James shifted his body and got his feet set, readying himself to take a swing at the girl with the wrench. He cursed himself for not still keeping his gun with him at all times, the way he did back in his active killer days, but he wasn't too worried. Should the day ever arrive where he couldn't easily handle a little thing like this bitch, he'd swallow a bullet and take his own ass out.

She came yet another step closer.

He smiled. "Damn. You must really want to die today."

In the next instant, he was distracted by a creaking sound from the back of the garage. He was tempted to glance in that direction, but the girl with the machete was so close now. If he let his guard down, she'd be able to rush forward and thrust the blade of the machete deep into his gut.

She came closer still.

The creaking from behind him got louder.

There was a door back there, an ordinary one with a window. James rarely locked this door and mostly used it for going out to the outdoor toilet. The hinges hadn't been oiled in decades, thus that terrible creaking sound. He hated to take his eyes off Machete Girl, but he needed to see what was happening at the back of the garage.

Backing off a couple quick steps, he glanced back there and saw another person coming into the garage, this one also wearing a mask, a white one with black hair attached. He scowled. Another fucking slasher mask. This new person was about as skinny as the girl, but was obviously male and a good bit taller. He was wearing a dark-colored jumpsuit of some kind. Gripped in his hands was a long-handled axe that looked newly purchased from a hardware store.

Then it hit him.

Mark.

He laughed and shook his head. "Oh, hell. It's you."

For a second there, he'd started getting a little scared.

He tossed the wrench on the table and hooked a thumb in the direction of the girl. "This your new piece?" He grunted. "I'd say you could do better, but you probably can't. Did she put you up to this stupid joke?"

The person he assumed was Mark raised the blade of the axe above the level of his shoulders as he came a few steps closer.

James glanced back and forth between them.

His frown returned.

Maybe he'd been too quick in tossing the wrench away.

They were continuing to inch closer, steadily reducing the space between them. A tingle of real fear went up his spine as he began to realize this wasn't a joke. They weren't playing with him. The intent here was lethal.

His hand darted to the table.

As soon as he did that, the girl came forward quickly, swinging the machete and burying the blade in the meaty part of his forearm. The pain was devastating, unparalleled by anything in his experience. He'd broken his wrist once in a bar fight, long ago. That was like being tickled by a feather compared to this. She ripped the blade away and blood gushed from the wound. The blade was swinging toward him again almost immediately. Dumb instinct caused him to raise his arm up in a defensive gesture. The blade cleaved easily through three of his fingers, sending them flying across the garage. More bright red blood geysered out of the stumps.

He staggered backward a step, dazed by pain and oblivious now to the secondary source of danger lurking right behind him.

Then the heavy blade of the axe punched deep into his shoulder, nearly taking off his arm.

He dropped to his knees.

His second attacker planted a heavy boot on his back and wrenched the axe free of flesh. Tears filled his eyes as more shock-waves of agony relentlessly lashed his body. The rest of it didn't take very long. They continued to hack away at him, keeping at it even after he'd collapsed to the floor.

The last thing he saw was the axe descending toward the middle of his face.

Mark dropped the axe and knelt next to his dead uncle. He peeled off his Michael Myers mask and handed it to Allison. She set it on the table and watched him as he studied the man's slack features in obvious disbelief.

He looked up at her, his eyes round with amazement. The smile on his face was like that of a kid after getting the thing he wanted most in the world for Christmas. "We did it. I can't fucking believe it. I'm finally free of this miserable son of a bitch."

Allison pushed her Jason Voorhees mask up to the top of her head.

A small smile appeared at the corners of her mouth. "I'm glad you got to have this moment. You deserve it."

He smiled.

He was still smiling when she rammed the machete blade into his throat.

She kept the blade lodged there a moment and watched the look on his handsome face change to an expression of surprise and pain. The transformation fascinated her. Her smile widened a little. She jerked the blade out and he fell onto his side as blood erupted from the severed big vein in his throat. Only after the blood slowed to a trickle and stopped did she turn away and walk out of the garage.

The walk back to her rented car took a while. It'd been necessary to park on a little used narrow dirt road nearly a mile away and approach James Castleberry's property on foot. Otherwise he would've heard them coming up his long driveway. This was what Mark had told her and she couldn't argue with his logic, especially now she'd seen the place, but it meant dealing with a fair amount of anxiety about being spotted by someone once she emerged from the woods and approached the car. She knew it was unlikely, but that didn't stop her from worrying.

The worry lessened considerably when she stepped through the line of trees and saw no other vehicles on the narrow lane. She dug the key fob out of her pocket and hit the button to open the trunk. She lifted the lid and wrapped the bloody machete in the cheap blanket she'd taken from the hotel room they'd stayed in last night.

It was a souvenir.

She planned to clean it and have Kane Hodder sign it the next time she saw him at a convention. The actor who'd portrayed Jason in four *Friday* movies typically sold his own custom machetes at appearances. They came with the edges dulled and edge-guards attached. She expected some grief over trying to get him to sign an alternate machete, but she was convinced she could talk him into it.

After thumping the trunk lid shut, she got in the car, started the engine, and started driving back down the road, away from James Castleberry's remote property and the corpses she was leaving there.

It'd been an eventful couple of weeks.

There was no denying that.

The cops showed up outside Cassie's apartment building within moments of Allison stashing the *Homecoming* tape away in her car. The cops knew nothing about the tape and therefore had no reason to search for it or ask her about it. She was not implicated in the deadly events of that day. The forensic evidence left no doubt as to the basic matter of who killed who. She was asked if she could guess why it had happened.

She told them she wasn't really sure.

It all happened right before she got there.

"Maybe a lover's spat," she said.

Mark was lurking near her house when she finally returned home hours later. Spooked by the sirens, he'd taken off, eventually summoning an Uber to drop him off in the vicinity of her neighborhood. She let him back into her house and they discussed everything that had happened and started plotting what to do next.

It was she who'd hatched the murder-revenge scheme against James Castleberry. The idea appealed to her because Mark's uncle sounded every inch like a man deserving of the most violent form of retribution possible. Arranging for them to die essentially together, however, gave her a clean slate.

Homecoming belonged to her alone now.

No one other than her would ever see it again.

She looked at the rearview mirror and this time she didn't scream or even flinch when she saw him in the backseat.

The man with the melting face.

The Visitor.

"We're connected now," she said breathily, a dreamy smile on her face. "I feel you inside me and I welcome you. With all my fucking heart, I welcome you."

He was her friend now.

The only one she'd ever need again.

She couldn't wait to see what gifts he might bring her.

BIO

Bryan Smith is the author of numerous novels and novellas, including *68 Kill*, *Slowly We Rot*, *Depraved*, *The Killing Kind*, and *Kill For Satan!*, which won a Splatterpunk Award for best horror novella of 2018. He won a second Splatterpunk Award in 2020 for *Dirty Rotten Hippies and Other Stories*. He is also the co-author of Suburban Gothic, written with Brian Keene. *The Infinity Engine*, a splatter western forthcoming from Death's Head Press, is due out in 2021. A film version of *68 Kill*, directed by Trent Haaga and starring Matthew Gray Gubler from *Criminal Minds*, was released in 2017. He lives in TN with his dogs Mac and Roxie.

A playlist for *The Unseen* can be found at:
https://open.spotify.com/playlist/2HnsdmHW3cW7ARxquUb56y
?si=f5ece6b6547040c8

Other Grindhouse Press Titles